A Dance W

An Irish Soldier of Fortune at the Little Bighorn

Lance J. Dorrel

A Dance With Death

"A man who defends his country or attacks another is no more than a soldier. But he, who adopts some other country as his own and makes offer of his sword and his blood, is more than a soldier. He is a hero."

~ Emile Barrault

Montana Territory
25 June 1876

"Where is the brave one?"

"He lies over the ridge, Sitting Bull," the warrior said and pointed east.

The Sioux war chief and his warriors slowly nudged their ponies up the hill and halted, gazing at the scene below. Dead soldiers lay strewn across the back side of a ridge. Indian warriors hollered as they stripped and mutilated the dead.

The warriors stopped their carnage and moved away from the dead as Sitting Bull approached a group of soldiers lying together in a clump. At the same time, a large contingent of Sioux and Cheyenne warriors appeared above the ridge. Their leader, Crazy Horse joined the war chief.

"Is that him?" asked Sitting Bull.

Crazy Horse had dismounted to see the soldier for himself. It appeared the soldiers had formed a square around this one before they all were killed. "Yes, that is him," he said. "He killed Cheyenne and Sioux." The warriors muttered amongst themselves and moved closer to see this soldier all talked of. "He fought like a grizzly. His eyes were like coal glistening with fire. When we cut the ridge, he covered his men. He did not run like the rest of the white soldiers."

More warriors had come. They followed a Sioux warrior by the name of White Bull, and had been in the fight against the soldier all wanted to see. "Where is his horse?" White Bull asked. "His horse fought as hard as he did."

Brave Bear, a Cheyenne warrior, who had fought the soldier and his men looked at the other Indians. "Yes, we should send his horse to him in his next life. He should have the horse with him."

"I want to know his name. This soldier who you say fought so hard and well," Sitting Bull said. Not only a war chief, but a holy man as well, Sitting Bull knew the importance of killing such a soldier. "Leave the horse for the other soldiers to find. Let him tell this tale."

Crazy Horse pulled a pair of gloves from the soldier's belt. He looked them over, unable to read the writing etched on the gloves. Finished with his inspection, he handed them to Sitting Bull.

The war chief read the name stitched into the fabric.

Myles Keogh

Part One

One

Myles Keogh wanted to experience the American West, and as the train carried him to the frontier, he anticipated a new adventure.

The train's whistle shrieked. "Knoxville!" called the conductor.

Keogh looked out the window at the station as his fingers ran over two objects clutched in his hand. He turned his palm up to look at the medals, then placed them back into his coat pocket.

As he walked the streets, Keogh wondered if he'd done the right thing. He had to thank his friend for the help in advancing his career, but the awkwardness of visiting unannounced bothered him. Still, he'd found his was way there. He hesitated outside the house to gather his thoughts and words.

The home was alive with company. Voices echoed out to him on the sidewalk as they talked and laughed. In the air, he smelt fresh bread and cooked beef.

Just go knock. You have to. This man helped you, for God's sake. You don't have any other friends.

Keogh knocked. No answer. He hands shook, but he knocked again.

Nothing. He picked up his bag and descended the steps. Now, he truly hoped no one would answer. Behind him the door squeaked open.

Damn.

"Sir, you knocked?" said the woman.

He turned and removed his hat. "Yes, I did. Good evening. My name is Myles Keogh." He walked back up the steps. "I am here to see Andrew Alexander."

"I see. My name is Emily Martin. Pleased to meet you." She offered her hand. "I'm Alexander's sister in-law. Please come in."

He stepped over the threshold and waited inside the entryway, unable to recall when he'd last set foot in a house. As he looked around the home, it occurred to him just how removed from ordinary life he had been, fighting in two wars, on two continents, in five years.

"Keogh, Myles Keogh!" shouted Alexander. "My God man, it's sure good to see you my friend."

All background noise ceased. Every eye was fastened on him. "I didn't mean to interrupt your night Alexander. I was passing through and wanted to say hello."

"Nonsense. Everyone, this is my good friend, Myles Keogh. We served in the war together."

A young woman appeared Alexander's side.

"Keogh, this is my dear wife Evy."

"Pleased to make your acquaintance Mister Keogh," Evy said. "I've heard much about you." She glanced at two woman who joined them. "These are my sisters. Emily, whom you have already met and this is my oldest sister, Nelly. We expected to see you at the wedding, did we not girls?"

Embarrassed, Keogh fumbled for the right words. "I do regret not making what I am sure was a grand affair. I had other obligations."

"Won't you please join us?" said Evy. "We have plenty of food."

"Yes, of course he will," Alexander said. "Let's have a drink and catch up while dinner is prepared."

The two friends moved to the porch. Alexander poured Keogh a bourbon. "So, you're heading out West, are you?" He handed Keogh the drink. "I am so sorry about O'Keefe."

"As am I, Alexander," Keogh sipped his drink. "No matter now."

"I wonder if Custer will remember you?" asked Alexander. "He reacts to situations, rather than forming a plan. He's reckless at times, but fearless."

Keogh knew General George Custer's story. Their paths had

crossed when both saw action in the Virginia theatre and at Gettysburg.

Known for having several horses shot out from beneath him when leading cavalry charges, Custer became a legend of sorts. He received a Brevet Brigadier General's rank to become one of the youngest generals in the history of the American Army. In a very short time George Custer became the best cavalry commander the Union Army had and an American hero. After the war, he was appointed command of the United States Seventh Cavalry.

"I always had a premonition my path and Custer's would cross again. Just never figured I'd be serving under him, in a cavalry regiment headed to the West. Thank you, Alexander, for helping me secure my commission."

"You are welcome, my friend. Any outfit would be lucky to have you in its ranks."

"I look forward to a new beginning. I've wanted to see the American West, heard some stories from those who served out that way and figured I'd see plenty of action, too."

"You know, Keogh, I could get you on here. You don't have to keep moving."

Keogh studied his empty glass. He understood what Alexander was saying. In the house, laughter from the others gripped his chest, emphasizing the loneliness that had been his constant companion over the last year. "The offer is tempting, but I want to keep soldiering while I am still able." His thoughts turned back to Custer and his new assignment. "How would you play it, Alexander? That is, if you were me, with him?"

"Don't wait for a situation to unfold. When you see it, hit it head on. He likes decisiveness in leaders, men not afraid to stand by their own actions."

"Dinner you two," said Emily.

~

It wasn't until Keogh was seated across from Nelly Martin that he realized how beautiful she really was. He tried not to stare. She was the oldest sister. Blue eyes and brown hair, her smile reassuring, inviting conversation. It had been so long since he'd set down to a meal in the company of others besides soldiers. He hoped he could remember his table manners and etiquette.

Lost in conversation with Nelly, he was surprised how two people who had just met, could have so much to talk about. He had to stop himself. Yet, no one seemed to mind. Emily and a young Army officer by the name of Upton were lost in their own flirtatious game. Evy smiled at Alexander, giving Keogh the approval to carry on. The moment was not lost on him, strange as it was to figure. Had he not gotten off the train, he'd never have known Nelly existed.

With dinner done, he was unsure of his next move.

"Alexander, help me with the dishes," said Evy.

"I'll help, too," Nelly offered.

"Not tonight, you won't," her sister answered. "Mr. Keogh could use some company."

Surprised again, he jumped at the chance. "Care for some air?" he asked.

Nelly pushed herself away from the table, grabbed her shawl and moved to the front door.

Desperate to start a conversation, Keogh wished he could think of something to say as they walked. He hoped he could hide just how nervous he was from her. As they continued onward, no matter how hard he tried, nothing seemed to come to mind.

"My sister says you come from Ireland, but came here from Italy," Nelly finally said.

"What else does your sister tell you about me?"

"She says you've fought at Antietam, Brandy Station, Gettysburg, and even been a prisoner of war. Is all that true?"

"Well, yes. I was at all of those battles, but that doesn't mean I was fighting in them."

"What makes a man leave his home to continuously fight in wars and tempt fate, Mister Keogh?"

"I don't know, really." He pondered the question. "I always wanted to be a soldier."

She nodded, then tilted her head without saying a word. The look she gave him made it clear she reasoned there was more.

How does she know?

"I wanted to be part of something big. Remembered for being a soldier so brave and courageous, the type stories are told of and books written."

I can't believe I just told her that.

Silence fell between the two for the rest of the walk. When they arrived back at the house, Nelly stopped outside the front door. She turned around and met his eyes. "Has it been worth it so far?"

He knew what she meant, but offered no reply. His guard had been let down enough.

~

Myles Keogh had more to tell, but he'd never been the boasting type. From a prospering Irish family, compared to many in the last half of the 19th Century in County Carlow, he'd been blessed with a privileged childhood.

A restless soul through his boyhood, he was fascinated by tales of knights and wars. His days were spent roaming the family land, pretending to be a knight protecting the countryside. Other days, he was a Crusader, bound for the Middle-East.

By 1860, at the age of twenty, he had been college educated and had secured employment and prospects in the banking industry. Yet, the mundane life never suited him, as he longed for adventure with a chance to prove himself. Keogh wanted to try soldiering.

His chance came when news spread across Europe of the Italian unification movement. Italy becoming a country threatened the Catholic Church and the Pope's sovereignty. The conflict captivated Keogh's interest the moment the local parish priest announced the Pope's need for able-bodied men to muster and fight if necessary on the Church's behalf. An urgency filled him, the need to leave his quiet life, the comfort of his family, for the hardships of a soldier's life. Keogh decided to cast his lot with the Papal Army, to keep Rome free from the Italian unification movement.

With little information to go on, mainly that the Papal forces were gathering in Vienna, Keogh left home.

At his first glimpse of the Irish Sea at Waterford, en route to join the Papal Army, Keogh also met the two men who would forever change his life. Their names were Dan Keily and Joseph O'-Keefe, and they too waited for passage to Vienna to fight on the Pope's behalf.

The pair studied Keogh, most likely wondering just what someone like him was doing in their midst. He wasn't running from the law, or a failed marriage. He didn't need to soldier to make a living. Keogh was simply going for the adventure.

Keily, the older of the two, was somewhat vague with his past, other than to tell he had served in the English Navy. He was all lean muscle and looked the type of fellow that neither ran from a fight, nor let someone else beat him to the first punch. Joseph O'Keefe was closer to Keogh's age and had been a policeman in Cork. As a policeman at such a young age, he carried himself with a quiet confidence that Keogh admired.

It was July, 1860, when Keogh and his two new friends reached Vienna. There, they enlisted. Men from Ireland, Germany, Spain, Switzerland and other parts of Europe had heard the Pope's calling and felt compelled to join up.

The three stood out among the other raw recruits in drilling and instruction. So much so, that each soon received officer's commissions. They were shipped with their fellow Irishmen to Ancona, Italy, as part of four Irish companies given the task of holding the port town. It was there the war began for them, as the Piedmontese, the forces intent on unifying Italy, lay siege to the Papal Army's fortifications.

The Papal forces would see action in a hurry, defending the town from first shelling, then land assaults. Keogh, his two friends, and the other troops fought valiantly, despite overwhelming odds, lack of supplies and having had very little training.

As the siege continued, it quickly became apparent the Papal defenders could not hold the town. Their only hope was relief from other Papal forces. However, no relief could be expected, the situation grew dire. Keogh, a young second lieutenant, found himself in charge of men who had never been soldiers before and, in some cases, were older than he.

Despite the hardship, low morale and fighting a lost cause, Keogh excelled at leading men in combat. Surrender or escape never crossed his mind. He and his two friends would see it through to the end.

Even as he witnessed death up close, Keogh felt as if he was living his own personal odyssey. At night, sitting around the campfires, he relished the camaraderie, as he listened to stories from the likes of Keily and others who had served in various units and seen action elsewhere.

For those Irishmen and the other Papal forces who decided to stay and stick it out, the end appeared early one morning when the Piedmontese army massed in overwhelming numbers. Waves of infantry hurtled toward the Irishman, in moving squares, determined to crush the defenders once and for all. When the three friends gazed out at the forces gathered for their demise, they had to have questioned their choice to stay.

The outcome and their fates were decided for them without further loss of life. Shelling by the Piedmontese before the final attack, hit the Papal forces ammunition supply. A fireball erupted, completely destroying the Papal forces ammunition reserves. The Piedmontese called off the attack and negotiations began for the surrender of the town.

After one month of fighting, the Papal forces surrendered. Keogh and his two friends had survived. And in that survival, the soldiering life had taken hold of Keogh; he wanted more of it. To America and the Civil War Dan Keily and Joseph O'Keefe went.

Myles Keogh wasn't about to be left behind.

~

The American Civil War was everything Keogh envisioned a war to be. Full of pomp and grandeur, with large campaigns and battles. Despite the war's violence and large numbers of casualties, he relished in its glory, taking part in some of the biggest battles. His Civil War service record, the places and campaigns he'd participated in, read like the stuff of legend.

While Keogh's career trajectory continued upward during the war, he'd had his share of close calls as well as tragedy. As he and Nelly Martin walked under the stars that night, it struck him just how much the war had taken from him. This was the harsh reality, the loss of so many close friends. In June of 1862, Dan Keily was wounded in action in Virginia and died in a battlefield hospital. Joseph O'Keefe was taken as a prisoner of war fighting at Brandy Station the following year.

Through northern Virginia and into Pennsylvania, Keogh's unit chased Confederates in route to Gettysburg. The whole way there, he desperately searched for O'Keefe, even contemplating leaving the Army to continue the search. But, his commanding officer, General John Buford, convinced him the search would be easier if he stayed on.

General Buford's horse troopers were very nearly overrun in defense of Gettysburg on day one of the fighting. Keogh played a significant part in the battle, running messages and directing artillery support close to retreating Union forces. Had it not been for Buford's units delaying the Confederate advance until Union Infantry arrived on the scene, the Battle of Gettysburg may have had a different outcome for Union forces.

Shortly thereafter, Buford succumbed to typhoid fever, leaving Keogh with yet another sense of loss. Later, while serving with the Army of the Ohio under General William Sherman, he rode in the campaign that cut through the deep South and marched to the sea. His beloved horse, Tom, was shot out from underneath him, as he took part in a botched attempt to free the Union prison camp Andersonville. With that attempt, Keogh himself became a prisoner of war.

While a prisoner of war in Charleston, South Carolina, Keogh contracted malaria. His health weakening daily, he feared he might die without proper medical treatment. The situation was compounded when Union forces lay siege to Charleston and their shelling landed dangerously close to the prison location.

But death was not ready for Myles Keogh. Having been traded in a prisoner of war exchange, he recovered and rose to the rank of Brevet Lieutenant Colonel by the war's end, a position which should have left him basking in glory. Instead, grief was all he knew at the news that Joseph O'Keefe had finally been freed in a prisoner of war exchange himself, only to stay on in service and be wounded again. When he found his friend, O'Keefe lay dying in a hospital. Keogh was at his side when he passed in May of 1865.

~

Keogh awoke before dawn. Unable to sleep, haunted with regret for letting Nelly see inside him, he was sure he'd scared her off. How could someone he just met understand how he felt? There were times even he was unsure why he continued soldiering after all he'd seen, all he'd lost. But the desire for more, to be more, always gnawed at him.

Besides, there was nothing to go home to. The truth of it was, he was scared to return home without more to his name. Scared he might never again see the West. Deep down, what drove him, was the thought of how there had to be more. It was his destiny to be part of something bigger than himself. Ireland could never offer him that. He was still a young man and a professional soldier. How many could say they had done and seen, let alone survived, all he had encountered?

His only hope was to leave without having to say an awkward goodbye. He'd write a note of thanks to all and be gone.

At the door he stopped to take one last look.

You will have a place like this to come home to someday.

"You leaving without saying goodbye, Mister Keogh?"

It was Nelly.

"I---I was just… No, of course not."

"Good, then I hope you'll join me for some breakfast. Do you like ham and eggs?"

~

They brought up the sun together. Complete strangers until the night before, they now talked and laughed as if they'd known one another for years. Keogh, for his part, had never known, let alone talked with a woman like this.

When the others in house began to stir, he knew his time with her was up. Waiting until the last possible minute, he moved to leave.

The awkward shyness with Nelly had passed. Now, it was only regret.

With goodbyes said to the rest, it was time he left. Keogh would walk alone to the train station, it was easier that way. If not, he feared he might stay.

At the gate, Nelly waited. "Myles, I have something for you." She handed him an envelope. "That is our home address, in Auburn, New York. I would be most honored if you were to write to me. That is, if you so wish?"

Surprised by her request, Keogh was reassured that his feelings had not betrayed him. He reasoned Nelly was as genuine a woman a man could hope to meet.

Say something.

Then it came to him. He reached into his coat pocket and pulled out a medal. "Nelly, would you keep this for me? To remember this time."

She looked at the medal, then smiled as she folded her hand around it. "I won't soon forget this time. What did you get this for?"

"Oh nothing." Keogh caught himself. He didn't want to diminish the importance of what the gift meant. "Where I'm going, well, I won't be needing it. This way, if something should happen to the other, at least you have one. They mean a great deal to me."

"You won't need an excuse to come visit me, Myles."

"Thank you." Keogh put his hat on, waived with his devil may care smile to those on the porch, then reached for Nelly's hand. He eyed the envelope. "With this, I shall talk to you. In my dreams, I hope we can take some more walks."

He turned onto the street, his steps light and measured. He was a man pursuing once again the great unknown. He looked at the remaining medal clutched in his hand.

Still bringing me good luck.

Alexander, Evy, and Emily walked to the gate. Nelly turned

over her hand to reveal what she had been given.

"My goodness," said Alexander. He took the medal. "I've seen that before. Not many men can say they ever got one of these. Two others, with medals like that, came with him. They got this fighting for the Pope."

"What about the others?" asked Evy.

"He and his two friends from Ireland. They all went to Italy to fight and then came over here to the war. He's the only one still alive."

Nelly listened as she watched Keogh disappear down the street.

Alexander handed her back the medal. "I wish he wouldn't go out there," he said. "He doesn't know just how brave he really is."

Two
November 1866
Kansas

His train had been on time. When it stopped at the makeshift Union Pacific Railroad depot, the train had traveled as far as the tracks ran on the Kansas frontier. As Keogh stepped off the platform, a vast sea of endless prairie grass stretched in all directions. The depot was busy and noisy as hundreds of men worked and moved all around, setting down new track.

Two soldiers stood and waited nearby with a wagon. Keogh moved in their direction. One stepped forward and saluted. He had a neatly trimmed mustache upon his weathered face, a set of broad shoulders carried a blue Army coat and his rank.

"Sergeant Hanrahan, sir."

"Captain Keogh, sergeant."

"Get the captain's bags, Lash."

The sergeant picked up the reins to the wagon. Keogh climbed on board and set next to him. Private Lash crawled up into the back of the wagon, grabbed his rifle and set with his legs hanging off the back.

"Ready, Lash?"

"Yes, sergeant."

With a flick of his wrist Hanrahan let the horses break into a trot. "Get up you two!" he said.

Through sun-browned prairie grass waiving from the wind off the plains, the two horse team pulled the wagon. Warmth shone down on Keogh and the two soldiers' faces, keeping them comfortable in the crisp fall air. They had five miles to cover to make Fort Hays.

Neither the sergeant, nor the private offered much in way of conversation. Keogh's eyes drifted to the fine rifle by the sergeant.

The weapon had drawn his attention from the moment he laid eyes on his new companions, as had the sidearm hanging about each man's hips.

"I see you both are armed and ready," said Keogh.

"And I see you are not, captain," Hanrahan answered, staring ahead at the horses.

Embarrassed at not being more prepared, Keogh said nothing in return.

The silence of the prairie was interrupted by the wagon's creak and the horses' snorting.

Hanrahan turned and looked Keogh up and down. "I can help you with getting armed captain." He faced ahead again. "Where you're going, you need to be armed all the time."

The wagon moved on. The blockhouse to Fort Hays appeared in the distance.

The fort was not what Keogh had envisioned one on the Plains to look like. There were no outer fortifications just the blockhouse distinguished it as a military post rather than some settlement. Troops and civilians moved freely about. Livestock covered the ground around the fort as far as a person could see.

Hanrahan pulled the wagon to a stop outside a wooden building. "Headquarters, captain. Lash, see to it that the captain's bags get over to the officers' quarters."

"Yes, sergeant."

"Get yourself checked in, captain," Hanrahan said. "I will find you after mess tonight. We'll get you squared away."

~

After dinner with the fort's officers, Keogh sat by himself outside the mess hall. The wind had picked up, and he stood, intending to grab his light coat from his quarters.

Once back outside, he was met by Hanrahan. "The post's sutler is a gunsmith, too. He charges an arm and a leg if you want the good stuff."

Keogh tilted his head. "If you were me, what would you do, sergeant?"

"If I was you, captain, going where you are, I'd damn well be sure I got the best guns I could buy. These here Army issued revolvers are Smith and Wessons. They'll knock a man down, that's for sure. The rifles they supply us with, ain't fit to even hunt with."

Hanrahan had moved on and Keogh followed. To the sutler's store, they went. The light from the inside shone through the window as the sergeant knocked.

The door squeaked as it opened. "Were closed, Hanrahan."

"I am sure you are. But this here officer, Captain Keogh to be exact, needs to make a purchase or two."

"Come back in the morning."

The door was pushed shut, but Hanrahan stuck his foot into the entryway to stop it. "Captain Keogh is headed for Fort Wallace, tomorrow. Besides, he was at Gettysburg."

The door went no further. The sutler stepped out of the store. He had a slight build, and his bald head glinted as brightly as the store light on his glasses. Keogh guessed the man to be in his fifties.

"Name's Neilson. Homer Neilson"

"Pleased to meet you," said Keogh.

"So you were there too?"

"I was."

"Did the sergeant tell you he was there himself?"

"No, he didn't."

"Well, come around back. Got stuff for you to see."

Behind the store, Neilson opened a padlocked door to a small shack. The lantern he carried glowed a dull yellow, illuminating the contents within.

The room contained several rifles, all cleaned and polished. Revolvers of all makes and brands lay about. There were so many, it was hard for Keogh to even know where to begin to look. He walked slowly among the guns and hoped the sutler and the sergeant would not pick up on his lack of knowledge when it came to the best weapons.

Neilson stepped forward. "Too many for a man to choose from. I understand." He moved to the rifles. "Here, take a look. I bet you've seen ones like this."

The rifle he handed Keogh was a Spencer Carbine, a definitively familiar make. The Army had issued these to the horse troopers Keogh served with at Gettysburg.

The weapon felt good in his hand, and he remembered just how powerful it could be.

"That's the best rifle I got," Neilson said. "It will last you forever as long as you take care of it."

"I'll take it. Show me the best revolvers you got."

Neilson moved among the weapons and grabbed two revolvers by their barrels. "Here you go."

The wood to the gun's handles was a dark brown. The barrel was a polished black and gray.

"Those will take the head off anybody that messes with you," said Neilson.

"How much for the guns and ammunition?" Keogh asked.

"You had better get him some extra ammunition, while you're at it," Hanrahan advised. The sutler and Keogh looked at the sergeant. "Might be sometime before you can get yourself back this way," he explained.

Neilson gathered two belts with holsters for the revolvers. Next, he grabbed boxes of cartridges.

"Here you go. This should keep you alive for some time over there." He handed Keogh the items, then went back for something else. "Here, on me."

The blade of a hunting knife gleamed in the dim lighting. Keogh pulled it from the scabbard.

"A man always can use a knife on the frontier," said Neilson.

"How much?"

"One hundred and fifty."

Keogh's eyes widened at the sutler's generosity. He handed Neilson the money. "Are you sure?"

"Of course I am."

"Thank you, Mr. Neilson. I will be forever in your debt."

"No need. Stop in again when you get back this way."

With his new guns in hand, Keogh and the sergeant headed back to the officers' quarters. Hanrahan said nothing as they walked, though Keogh could sense something was on his mind. "Why did he give me such a deal?" he asked.

"I think he felt sorry for you, that's all."

Keogh stopped walking. "Is it really that bad over there?"

The sergeant looked him in the eye. "Captain, find the scouts and frontiersman over there. All I can tell you is to listen and learn all you can from them. It's a different kind of fighting out here."

"Thank you, Hanrahan. I will." The two resumed their walk. "I still can't get over him giving me these guns and such, at the price he did."

"His son rode with the Illinois Cavalry."

"Is he still in the Army?"

"He was killed at Gettysburg."

Three
Fort Wallace
Kansas

"Where is the commanding officer, soldier?" asked Keogh.

The young private stood at rigid attention. "Lieutenant Bates is out with the hay cutting crew, sir."

"Tell me, private, where are the officers' quarters?"

The private pointed out the window to a group of wood buildings.

Keogh looked around the small building. He couldn't believe it was the Adjutant's Office, used as the command center to Fort Wallace. The fort was the westernmost outpost on the Kansas frontier for the United States Army. "Get me an orderly on the double."

"Sir?"

"I am taking over command here. I am Captain Keogh, Seventh Cavalry." He picked up his bags and headed for the officer's quarters.

"Right away, sir."

Outside the office, a strong wind off the prairie hit him. He surveyed the fort. The harsh reality of his situation sank in the more he studied his new post. Most of the buildings looked to be in disarray and in need of some type of repairs.

What was considered officers' quarters were in reality, nothing more than crude wood shacks. There was no stove. A small table and a couple of chairs, to go along with a bedframe, were all the furnishings.

"Sir, reporting as ordered," said the trumpeter.

"At ease. What is your name?"

"Clarke, sir."

"Well Trumpeter Clarke, you and I are going to get to know

each other real well. Do you understand me, Clarke?"

"Yes, sir."

"Good. Now find every officer this place has. I want them to report to me, six o'clock sharp, mess hall."

~

Keogh purposely waited until five minutes after the hour before he addressed the officers. His entrance was to be seen by all. He had to gage those interested, from those not fully vested.

At his arrival, all stood at attention. "At ease," Keogh said. All continued to stand. "As you were."

They were an assorted bunch, these officers stationed at Fort Wallace. Some with the Seventh Cavalry, others were infantry officers from the Third and Thirty-Seventh Regiments.

Keogh listened to their reports. What stood out the most to him was the fact that the horses had no shelter for the oncoming winter. The enlisted men had only tents. Wood for the heating and cooking had to be brought from the river, two miles away. Stoves had arrived, but as of yet, no stove piping. He felt anxious and uneasy at the thought of how miserable and cold it would be once winter set in if something was not done to improve the fort's quarters for men and animals.

Lieutenant Bates report was short and to the point. The fort was garrisoned by five depleted companies of the Seventh Cavalry. Keogh commanded I Company and Captain Albert Barnitz G Company. Three lieutenants were the only other cavalry officers there with the two infantry companies hosting a lieutenant apiece.

Bates finished with more disheartening news. "Our muster rolls are incomplete. Duty rosters and daily logs are non-existent."

"Just how can that be?" Keogh asked.

"Desertion has plagued this post from the outset," answered Bates. "We have been so short of troops, protocol was just to let them be. If a trooper does desert, most comeback, for they can't even find their way out on the prairie."

The seriousness of the situation was apparent. Keogh thought of his next words carefully.

I didn't come all this way to be ruined by this hell hole.

"Barnitz, you are in charge of duty rosters, changing of the guard and all other duties associated with disciplinary matters, until further notified."

"Understood, captain."

Keogh scanned the men's faces, searching for a sign. Anything to reveal that one of these men wanted change. "You there, what's your name?"

"Lieutenant Beecher, sir. I am the acting quartermaster."

"Good. I want some form of stables for the horses, now, understood?"

"With pleasure, sir."

"For the rest of you, I want your company rosters and report on arms. Any questions?"

A tall soldier in a tailored uniform stepped forward. "Excuse me, sir. I have just reported to the post, sir. Might I know where I might be assigned, sir?"

One not yet jaded by the place. Here you thought all was bad.

"What is your name soldier?"

"First Lieutenant Henry Nowlan, sir."

There was a familiar sound to the soldier's words. Keogh knew he recognized something in the accent. "Tell me, just where is home, Nowlan?"

"England, sir."

A loud thud sounded from behind Keogh. He flinched. Caught off guard for a moment, and turned to find a huge deer carcass at his feet. Beside him stood a man in buckskin clothing, his right hand resting on a holstered revolver. His left hand hovered over a knife in a beaded scabbard. A wide brimmed hat sat on a head full of long black hair.

"So, you're the new commander, huh?"

"I am. The name is---"

"Don't give a lick about your name." He shook his head disgusted. "You forgot to ask them about something, didn't you?"

What is he referring to?

"Christ almighty. You sons of bitches are just plain ignorant. Just where in the hell do you think you are? Maybe you should ask about any reports of Indian activity!"

Embarrassed, Keogh searched for something to say. "Being that I am the new commanding officer, would it be too much of me to ask you your name?"

"I don't give a damn what you do."

For a moment, Keogh's blood began to rise. He'd learned from two wars to harness his temper and show nothing. "I didn't catch it…your name, that is?"

"Name's Comstock. William Comstock," he said and walked out the mess hall door.

"Wait, Comstock." Keogh followed.

The scout had mounted his horse, an Appaloosa.

"Comstock, I was hoping you might stick around." Keogh stuttered, looking around the barren prairie.

"No thanks, captain." He turned the horse.

Don't let him get away. Think.

"Could you give me the lay of the land? Maybe tomorrow?"

The horse stopped. The scout didn't turn around in the saddle. He slumped and rested his arms on the pommel. "Can you even ride a horse?"

He had a chance--- "Yes, I can ride."

Comstock pulled the horse around, then stopped the Appaloosa just short of Keogh. The scout leaned forward. "Why should I care?"

The man's look said plenty. Keogh could see Comstock's frustration. "Look, I chose of my own free will to come out here. I want to live it, not be killed by it."

A smile spread over Comstock's face. "You had better get this place in some type of order." The scout looked around the post, then up at the sky. "Winter coming on. You got about a month before it hits."

"These men here, they want change. We can make this fort better," said Keogh.

"You know you are constantly being watched?"

Keogh gazed out at the dark prairie. He felt vulnerable and exposed by the fort's starkness. It was engulfed by the vast prairie. "What tribe?"

"There's more than one." Comstock nodded. "You got a lot to learn."

"I'm willing."

"Tell you what. You get this place and those sorry sacks of shit running around here in some order, then we can talk. Until then, you had better thank your luck winter is coming on. Least this way they won't run you out until spring, maybe summer." Comstock pulled the Appaloosa to the right. "At least you're carrying a gun."

Keogh put his hand on the revolver.

Hanrahan.

Four
February 1867

Keogh woke to a black winter dawn. The room, cold and dark, only intensified his loneliness.

Get up and get moving.

He threw some wood into the stove and managed to stoke the last embers back to life. On his small desk, the letter to Nelly waited, not yet finished.

The two had kept a torrid pace of writing to one another ever since meeting. Keogh had even managed a short trip to visit her home in New York.

He splashed some cold water over his face, then moved out the door.

"Up and at it early, I see."

He jumped back in surprise and pulled his revolver. "Jesus Christ, Comstock! You're lucky I didn't shoot you."

The scout sat in the lone porch chair, outside Keogh's quarters. "Just where you going to shoot?"

What does he mean?

"Lesson one. When fighting Indians, shoot where you think he's going, not where you believe him to be." Comstock stood and finished his coffee. "Forget all you know about fighting. You got to think like an Indian."

They stepped off the porch. A revolver's hammer cocked from behind Keogh.

Comstock turned. "Lesson two. Where there's one Indian, going to be more. When fighting Indians, you got to move on them. You got to be able to ride and fight like a Comanche, if you got any hope of surviving a tangle with the likes of the Sioux, Cheyenne or Arapahoe. Stand around, and they'll hit you from all directions. Take the fight to them. They don't like it."

The scout began to speak in a form of Indian dialect Keogh had not yet heard. A click told him the hammer on the revolver had been lowered.

Out of the blackness stepped an Indian in a blue Army coat. His hair was in a scalp lock, perfectly cut down the middle of the warrior's head.

"This here is Blue Hawk. He is Pawnee. Sworn enemy to the Sioux and Cheyenne."

"What's with the Army coat?"

"So none of your fellows shoots them."

"What do you mean by them?"

"I got more Pawnees coming down to help us. It's going to be a long, hard summer Keogh." Comstock resumed walking. Near the stables, he turned to the two men. "Lesson three, and listen real well now." He stepped closer to Keogh. "Any man, Indian, white, Mexican, you name them, ever pulls down on you, you damn well better be prepared to finish them. It don't matter if you're an officer or in an Army coat. You understand me? Out here, it's kill or be killed. You better damn well remember that one. If not, you won't be getting another lesson!"

~

Keogh had much to learn if he was going to command soldiers on the frontier.

Comstock started with the basics. He taught Keogh how to hunt game without giving away his position, start a fire out of nothing, read the weather and find shelter.

A good shot with a rifle when dismounted and a revolver when astride a horse, Keogh was still lectured on the need to master it more. Comstock drilled in him to never leave post without being well armed, including carrying multiple revolvers on a horse.

As part of his new duties as post commander, Keogh had to

buy horses for the Army. Relay stations manned by troops and constant patrols protecting the stage line required huge numbers of horses. It was important he get it right. Comstock and the Pawnees showed him what to look for in a good horse.

The Pawnee Indian scouts brought in by the Army taught him how to track an elusive enemy and how to read the signs the frontier gave up. The scouts educated Keogh on recognizing what tribe was in the area by reading the signs they left behind.

The area in and around Fort Wallace was a crossroads to many Plains Indian tribes. The Indians followed the buffalo herds, which now came near the new settlements and crossed paths with wagon trains moving west.

From the Pawnee, Keogh learned how to fight. Indian methods were different, but he quickly adapted. The scouts made sure he knew how to use his knife, if needed.

It was imperative that he immerse himself in Plains Indian culture. Smart enough to learn the basics of sign language, Keogh made it a priority to communicate with Indian bands as they traveled in and around the fort to learn each tribe's customs and ways.

Over time, he became skilled enough to survive on his own in the rugged land. Comstock and the scouts had been good teachers. Now, Keogh was a Plainsman. It was up to him to use all he had learned to keep himself and his men alive.

Five
Summer 1867

"Easy you two," whispered Keogh. He fed his two horses some grain and oats. Not fully trusting the care of his horses to the new recruits or others, he welcomed the quiet time in the evening with Paddy and Mary Jo. "How's my girl?"

Mary Jo had caught his attention during his first trip to the stables when he took over as commander of the fort. None of the other officers thought much of her. When he walked by, she kept nudging him with her nose. Black, with a white swath down the middle of her face, Mary Jo served as his horse when scouting and chasing raiding Indian war parties.

Not big by Army standards, Mary Jo would go into any ravine and climb with the best. Keogh had never ridden a mare before and was surprised at her instincts and fearlessness on the trail. She was eager and happy he knew to be with him, even when out after Indians. She was still only five years old and he loved her. It didn't take long for worry to set in. She was his girl, but fights would soon be inevitable. The time had come to find another horse for fighting Indians.

Paddy was thought to be a thoroughbred, least that's what Comstock surmised. The horse was lean muscle and bigger than a mustang. Comstock and the Pawnees found him alone, the only survivor of an ambushed wagon train. How and why the horse was not taken, was a mystery. The scouts gave the horse to Keogh as a gift.

Most of the time Keogh rode Paddy around the fort's grounds and surrounding area when he wanted to be alone and think of Nelly. When he did let the horse run, it was as if the two rode the Kansas wind.

Life at Fort Wallace had improved for the men serving there.

As Keogh walked to the mess hall, he looked around the fort feeling more secure for the next winter. At least the horses had stables, there was an infirmary, and all the post buildings had been reinforced with plastered adobe. Most buildings had wooden porches. Log barracks with stoves served the enlisted men. The makeshift shack that had once served as the Adjutant's Office, had been replaced by a brand-new building that was up to Army regulations.

"Captain, a minute if you please?" said Lieutenant Nowlan.

One of Keogh's first actions as commanding officer had been to make Nowlan the post Adjutant. A veteran of the Civil War, Nowlan had served in the English Army before coming to America. Keogh trusted him and knew he'd made his life and the post better.

"Let's get some coffee," Keogh said.

They entered the mess hall after the night's dinner had been served. Various officers clustered around the tables. Keogh felt lucky to have this group stationed with him. It was because of them, he knew, the fort had become something to be proud of.

The post doctor, Turner, was busy informing Captain Barnitz and his First Sergeant, Frederick Wyllyams, on the condition of some of their company's troopers. Lieutenants Hale and Cox sat close, waiting for the doctor's report on their men.

Comstock sat with Lieutenants Beecher and Bell. Beecher was the character of the group and the best junior officer Keogh had. Tough, fearless and with merits from the war to prove his bravery, Beecher at times was reckless when on the trail chasing Indians.

At the table by Comstock, Keogh and Nowlan settled.

"You straightening Beecher out on the dangers of not using flankers?" asked Keogh.

"Hell, he ain't the only one around here not listening. You would think some of these fellows got themselves memory problems," Comstock said and pointed his cup at Sergeant Wyllyams. "If some of the Pawnees hadn't been with him and his company, you'd be burying the lot."

"Captain, please. A word, if you don't mind?" pleaded Nowlan.

"Yes, my apologies. You were telling me?" Keogh asked.

"General Custer has been relieved of field command of the Seventh by Sheridan and Hancock," said Nowlan.

"Go on."

"Major Elliot has been appointed field commander for now," Nowlan announced.

The room fell quiet. All listened.

"Well," said Comstock. "Custer can't catch any Indians. Then he decides to abandon his men, cause he's hard up for his woman. Tried to say he was afraid she might get the cholera. Serves him right."

"Do you have more?" asked Keogh.

"Yes, captain. Over the wire, the War Department from Leavenworth sent out the stipulations to the most recent treaty," Nowlan continued.

"And?"

"Well, it states the Sioux are to stay north of the Platte. The Cheyenne are to vacate this part of the state. They are to stay south of the Arkansas. General Hancock wired all posts to be ready to take the field early next spring, to drive any bands not following the treaty back to their designated grounds," reported Nowlan.

"Better get some more horses," Comstock advised. "Looks like a war is about to happen."

Six
September 1867

"It's a good thing we are getting new horses," said Nowlan. "If we had to ride these poor creatures back to Wallace, we'd probably be walking most of it."

"What do you expect, Nowlan?" Beecher asked. "Hell, we've chased Indians from Wallace all the way down to the Arkansas River. Now, the captain has got us headed for Hays."

At the head of two tired and dust covered companies of the Seventh, Keogh rode Mary Jo. Plodding along next to him was Comstock with Pawnee scouts and a few troopers. The scouts looked for signs of Cheyenne, Arapahoe or Sioux raiding parties. They hoped to strike a fresh trail before crossing the Smokey Hill River.

"You know what gets me about chasing these damn Indians?" Beecher said. "We chase them from one station or homestead, to another. We never really know which way they've gone or where they're going to hit next. Then, out of the blue, it's as if they've left us a trail of sorts. Almost like they want us to follow and find them."

The exhausted men slumped in their saddles as they continued toward Fort Hays.

"Beecher, why do you think the Indians want us to find their signs?" asked Comstock.

Keogh listened intently. He needed his junior officers to understand the dangers when chasing Indians.

"Don't ever forget this," Comstock said. His Appaloosa walked beside Beecher's horse. "Make no mistake about who or what we are chasing out here, boys," he stated. "These so---called savages, are hunters and warriors as smart and cunning as any men who ever walked the earth. The signs are so we go head long right into a trap. An Indian is born to fight. It's how he gains honor and standing among his people."

Fort Hays was the center hub to a succession of Army forts, built throughout Kansas. Located near the Smokey Hill River, as well as the railroad, the fort was bigger than most. It served as a destination point for numerous Army patrols, settlers moving west and a central depot for new horses acquired by the Army.

The fort's commanding officer gave Keogh the latest Indian activity report and other small talk related to Army matters. "Major Elliott is on his way here, Keogh," said the captain. "You beat him. He's coming for horses, too."

Several recruits, along with one blacksmith, went about the business of breaking and shoeing the new horses, though some had more luck than others. None of the new horses wanted any part of it.

The group Keogh looked for had positioned themselves against the fence of the huge corral. "We'd better hurry. More companies coming in for horses," he said.

Comstock asked the sergeant in charge, "Where did they get this bunch?"

"I was told they come from the Indian Territory."

They studied the horses for some time before Comstock went about choosing the best he'd seen.

Keogh chose a few and kept an eye out for one he might keep for himself. Much to his disappointment, none stood out from the others. He was ready to move on when a bay, standing off from the others, caught his eye.

The horse was a clay bank color with black feet. There was nothing physically imposing about the animal. Keogh had certainly seen bigger, but the horse was all compacted muscle. Still, he watched the horse. As new recruits and others went by, the horse repeatedly neighed and shook his head at each.

The poor animal must be crazy.

The more he watched the horse, the more apparent it became that the horse was not crazy, but very intelligent.

He's telling any who come close, they'd better not. He's giving all fair warning. You mess with me, and there will be hell to pay. Now, that's a horse worth taking a chance on.

Keogh approached the horse in plain sight. He walked directly in front of the animal and then stopped a few feet from it. "Easy boy, easy. I am not going to hurt you."

The horse looked him dead in the eyes, let out a neigh and shook his head. It was as though he was asking, "What in the hell are you looking at?"

Astonished, Keogh froze.

What a horse of character this is.

"I will take this bay, sergeant. See that he is ready to go when we leave day after tomorrow."

~

"You beat us to the best. Damn you, Keogh," said Captain Frederick Benteen. The captain pulled off his gauntlets and extended his hand.

Senior Captain in the whole Seventh Cavalry, Benteen was the standard to which the rest of the officers measured themselves against. With a healthy head of wavy white hair set above blue eyes, he looked every part the rugged cavalryman. With more cavalry battles in the war than any other officer in the regiment, Benteen was the best the Seventh had in terms of a field commander. A quick learner to frontier Indian fighting ways, he was cautious but relentless when on the trail.

"Good to see you my friend," Keogh said.

"You, as well Keogh."

"I heard Elliott is on his way."

"I brought him. He's a nice change, compared to the boy general." Benteen took off his wide-brimmed field hat and slapped the dust from his Army pants. "He don't feel men and horses are disposable, like Custer does."

Major Joel Elliott approached the two. "There you are Keogh. I've heard you got Wallace in top shape. You're being noticed, captain."

Joel Elliott had served with distinction in the Civil War. A native of Indiana, he was calm and reserved, but his personality changed when fighting. Aggressive and ready to fight when on the trail, Elliott led from the front. The troopers respected him and the officers in the Seventh were pleased he'd been given command during General Custer's suspension.

"Thank you, sir. Indian activity has been rather quiet," Keogh said.

"That will change once they're given notice of the treaty. Be prepared for a spring campaign," Elliott warned. "Hancock is itching to go out and Custer will be back."

The talk of a spring campaign reminded Keogh of his intentions. "I am requesting leave, just over Christmas, sir."

Elliot smiled. "Go on."

"One month's leave, sir. I'll make it a priority to be back long before spring hits," he offered.

"Put it in writing, Keogh. I'll pass it on up."

Seven
December 1867
Auburn, New York

As he stepped off the train her voice, so soft and loving, floated to him over the sea of passengers.

Nelly

"Myles. Myles Keogh!" Nelly called and waved. "Here I am Myles."

He dropped his bags to the ground and she quickened her steps. When the two were close, she reached for his hand.

"Nelly. It's sure good to see you."

"You as well Myles. You're as handsome as the last time I saw you."

"And you are more beautiful than before."

"Let's go home, Myles. Much is happening."

The sprawling estate that was the Martin family home was called Willowbrook. Located in western New York, the home set just outside of Auburn. A perfect array of snow had blanketed the countryside.

More at ease on his second visit to Nelly and her family, Keogh so looked forward to the holidays. He would stay in the guest house, as all rooms in the mansion were needed.

A wedding was taking place---Emily and Emory Upton.

The next weeks were more peaceful and soothing to Keogh's soul than any other time in his life. It was all he had dreamed and hoped for. The Christmas wedding added to the holiday spirit.

Keogh's days were spent talking with family members and friends of the Martin family about the West. So many were interested in Nelly's guest, the young cavalry officer with his stories of Indians and fighting. Afternoons, though, were spent with Nelly. They walked the grounds and traveled the countryside.

Evenings were magical. A big family supper, followed by the whole group retiring to the massive library. Keogh's stories entertained all. The oversized fireplace was kept ablaze and, at the crackle of burning embers, Keogh's journey was easy to imagine.

Few could have imagined the scenes he described, the adventure and the cast of characters he'd encountered up to this point in his life. He portrayed himself as just an average soldier, but to those listening, it was easy to see he was much more. Myles Keogh was daring and bold, not someone afraid of the unknown. It was just the way he wanted himself to be seen.

Keogh hated for his visit to end. On his final day, he and Nelly slipped away for a walk around the grounds.

She was reserved, more so than she had ever been in his presence. She walked some distance ahead of him for most of it. To him she seemed to be preoccupied with something. He could sense her mood was serious.

"Myles, when will I see you again?"

He could not give her an answer, as he truly did not know.

"What becomes of us now?" she asked. She grabbed his hand, then rested her head on his shoulder.

Unsure what to do, Keogh hesitated. He'd not even the courage to attempt a kiss. "I don't want to leave, Nelly. This time I've spent here with you and your family has been wonderful. I'm not sure why any man would not want to spend the rest of his life here with you. But I want to see the West before it's gone. I hope you understand." He stared into her eyes. "You have changed me, and now I have something in my life that I feared I would never find."

His last night with Nelly passed quickly and Keogh tried to take it all in. He found himself drifting in and out of his thoughts at the dinner table. Each time, he obsessed over the same question.

Why leave her and all this?

When he finally left Nelly for the night he was sad and lonely.

He didn't want to go to bed and contemplated going back to the main house to see her. For the longest time he just set in the dark, lost in his thoughts.

After he'd dozed off, a timid knock sounded at his door. At first, he thought he was hearing things. Then it came again. He got out of the bed, slipped into his pants, and opened the door. "Nelly, what are you doing here?"

She stood before him, draped in only her nightgown and a shawl. Her hair hung past her shoulders, and she was barefoot. "I have come to give myself to you, Myles Keogh."

She entered and closed the door behind her. Without a word she led him back to the bedroom, pushed him down onto the bed, then backed away. Silent, she stood there. He could see her figure perfectly in the winter moonlight. Nelly dropped the shawl and slowly lifted her nightgown off her body.

He could find no words to speak.

She stayed with him the entire night. As the two laid in bed, he watched her as she slept. "Nelly, you must get up. You have to go back to the house, before your family wakes."

"Stop your worrying." She placed her hand on his face. "I know my family after all these years."

He studied her features carefully, wanting the memory of her burned into his mind. For the first time in his life, he'd found a woman who captured his heart.

Nelly was strong, self-assured---- her own person. He loved that about her. The fact she was devoted to her family and to their care, appealed to him.

Afraid to fall asleep, he continued staring as the night gave way to early morning. He feared waking and her having slipped away. "Nelly, Nelly," he whispered. "Are you sleeping?"

"Not anymore. Go to sleep my love."

"I can't Nelly. I don't want to forget what you look like."

"Then I will see you in your dreams."

A thought crept into Keogh's mind.

You may never see her again. Why do this to yourself?

Then the reality of his situation returned.

Even if you decide to leave the Army, you still have to finish out your time. You are a soldier. It is your calling, your destiny.

How could he ever reconcile his destiny with his love for Nelly?

You cannot drag her into your humble existence. You cannot do that to her. A soldier has a duty, and you took an oath to the Army of the United States of America. It is who are. It may not be much, Myles Keogh, but it is all you have.

It was all he could offer Nelly and, to him, it was not enough.

~

At the first signs of dawn, Nelly slipped away.

Keogh woke to an empty bed, the feeling of warmth and love quickly replaced by the apprehension of returning to the Army, of saying goodbye.

Already lost in his thoughts of what to say, he headed to the main house in the early morning darkness. Once inside, he smelt breakfast. Fresh bread, the eggs and ham.

Just like the first time she cooked breakfast for me.

An uneasy sensation that caused his stomach to churn worked through him. He knew he must give her some reassurance. He'd never expected to find someone like her, he wanted her in his life. Yet, he struggled between offering her all he had and still yearning to leave his mark on the world.

In the hallway Keogh stopped and secretly watched Nelly as she prepared breakfast in the kitchen.

She noticed him and blushed. "How long have you been standing there?"

"Not long enough."

"Sit down so we can eat. I still have to get ready afterwards," she said.

She rode with him to the train station. The morning air, cold and sharp, misted before them each time they drew breath. Her silence through the ride troubled him. Of course, he remained quiet, too, lost for what to say.

When the wagon stopped, Nelly turned to him. "I need you to come back to me, Myles, and I need to know when that will be."

Tears streamed down her cheeks. Keogh fumbled with the reins to the wagon, hastily retrieving his handkerchief to gently wipe away her tears. He kissed her and tasted the salt on her skin. There were no words to ease her pain.

Keogh looked at his watch. Only twenty minutes left with her if the train was running on time. They found a bench outside the ticket office and waited together. As he held her hand, he summoned the courage to speak. Where his words came from, he did not know. "Nelly, my enlistment will be up in three years. If you are willing to wait on me, then we---"

The shaking of her head stopped him. "No, Myles, no! You stupid, stupid man. Do you think I would bring you here--- sleep with you, only to wait three more years? You can't do this to me anymore! Do you hear me?"

Her tone was like a slap to his face, the anger in her voice a brand.

"I can't wait on you and worry if you're even going to make it back to me alive." She stood from the bench.

The approaching train's whistle let out a lonely shriek.

"What do you want me to do, Nelly?"

She turned from staring at the tracks and looked directly into his eyes. The gaze of a woman in distress. Sadness, then a sense of loneliness washed over him.

"I want you to let my father and my uncle get you out of the Army. You belong here with us. If you love me, Myles, you will do this for me. I don't know why you want to go back there where Indians can out fight you, where death awaits a man at every turn. No, you come back here, so we can start our lives together."

She fell into his arms, sobbing. Keogh held her against his chest, praying for the right words. The train made its way into the station and stopped. He pulled back, staring fondly into her face. "I just can't right now, Nelly. You have to let me finish out my time, and then I'll come back to you."

Nelly swallowed hard, stepped back from him, and wiped away her tears. The train let out an enormous shriek. "I was afraid of that. I knew I couldn't make you stay, no matter what."

His heart sank, a hard stone in his gut. "Nelly, please. Just listen."

"No, you listen to me, Myles Keogh, and you listen good! I love you, and I will love you like no other woman can. We can have a wonderful life here. You think I'm going to spend these next three years waiting and worrying about you while I should be having a family?" She stopped herself. She knew she'd said enough---

"All aboard!" called the conductor.

Keogh picked up his bag and looked at the train. He turned back to her. "Nelly, just wait, please. I'll write you and come visit when I can. Maybe I can get out a little sooner than expected. Please wait on me. I will come back. Please, Nelly! Please."

The train lurched forward. Keogh pulled her against his chest and kissed her. Nelly was emotionless. He stepped back. All he could do was look at her, nothing left to say. He had to go, there was no more time. The train was moving as he threw his bag to a conductor standing on the steps. Keogh jumped on board and turned to wave at Nelly one last time. She was not there. As the train pulled him away and back to Kansas, time had run out on him.

Eight
Summer 1868
Fort Wallace

Finished with the letter, Keogh moved to make his morning rounds. Back on duty at Fort Wallace, he tried to busy himself with his duties, but he could not forget Nelly. Why did he bother sending another? She'd not responded to the previous two.

His first stop, the Adjutant's office. Keogh needed to check the daily reports and logs. On his he way, the changing of the fort's guard was being conducted, and a relief detail was leaving for the relay stations. Led by First Sergeant Wyllyams, the detail had three stations to make before the afternoon.

Keogh saw more activity, a company of infantry with wagons prepared to leave the fort. They were on duty this day to guard over the beef herd, being put out to graze west of the fort.

Trumpeter Clarke bounded out of the Adjutant's office and right into Keogh. "Captain, Lieutenant Nowlan sent for you. He says to bring you on the double."

In the Adjutant's office Keogh found Comstock drinking coffee with Nowlan. "What's so important, that I can't even get breakfast?" he asked.

This came from Fort Larned," said Nowlan. "Hancock and Custer attacked and put the torch to a Cheyenne village, down on Pawnee Creek."

"I knew Hancock and Custer had gone that way for negotiations," Keogh said. "Wonder what caused them to attack?"

"You can't reason with Dog Soldiers," Comstock told. He finished his coffee and stood. "Going to be a restless and tough summer, Keogh. "I thought they might try to run you out last year, but now I am sure of it. They will come soon, mark my words."

"Maybe General Custer will catch up with those Dog Soldiers

and put an end to them, once and for all," Nowlan said.

"Custer has no chance of finding any Dog Soldiers," stated Comstock. "They'll find him if they want to fight."

"And there lies the problem, doesn't it?" Keogh said, as he looked out the window towards the prairie. He took a drink of his coffee. "Now us and everyone in between the Arkansas and the Platte is going to pay for it!"

"I have taught you well, Keogh," smirked Comstock. "Now, let's get some breakfast."

~

First Sergeant Frederick Wyllyams led the detail across the endless prairie. Even at a trot, the horses kicked up clouds of dust. From Fort Wallace they rode east against a dry and chaffing wind. With their hats pulled down low, the horse troopers tried to shield their eyes against the sun, almost ever-present during the summer months on the Plains.

The detail was on time so far, as they dropped ten enlisted men and one non-commissioned officer at the Downer's Creek and Chalk Bluff relay stations along the Smokey Hill River. He pushed his ten remaining troopers hard, for the station at Monument Rocks. They had to get there and relieve the previous detail, in order to give them time to get back to Fort Wallace. Wyllyams had served on the frontier for a number of years now and was experienced enough to know night on the prairie, for such a small party of troopers, could be a death sentence.

Set up by the Butterfield Overland Stage Company, the relay stations kept fresh horses and served as a rest stop for passengers. Most stations had an assortment of buildings: living quarters for the station attendees, a place for passengers to get a meal, sparse quarters for Army troops, stables and corrals for livestock.

Established within close proximity to fresh water, the stations had supplies and wood on hand. They were vital to stagecoaches and the wagon trains moving west with settlers. When the Army took over guarding the stations two years ago, Indian raids along the river trail ceased.

~

Kern Grimes rested against his infantrymen's long rifle. He was tired from guarding the beef herd and other livestock in the summer heat. The young private had wandered off from his fellow soldiers. The others were happy to be on such mundane duty and away from Fort Wallace. Once the herd was put out and the pickets placed, most ducked out of view for a nap or a game of cards.

Grimes moved back over the hill, towards the wagon and the rest of his company. He needed some coffee. A few steps more, and the private froze. Horses running, and not just a few. Movement at the corner of his right eye sent goosebumps across his body. He was being watched, he was certain of it. The livestock bellowed, their hooves pounding the dirt. Raising their heads, they smelled something--- or someone. Grimes scanned the terrain. None of the other soldiers from his company were visible. He quickened his steps for the wagon.

~

Monument Rocks Station was quiet as afternoon settled over the valley. The station was nestled between the river on one side and to the other, just a ways past the horizon, a series of huge rock formations resembling a broken down castle. The area near the river was a popular overnight spot for wagon trains.

Wyllyams squad had made good time. Sergeant Erving Drummel and his men, whom they relieved, would still have all evening to return to Fort Wallace.

While the incoming troopers dismounted and unsaddled, those about to leave went about preparations for their own journey.

"Any activity or troubles?" Wyllyams asked.

"Quiet as church," said Drummel.

Wyllyams looked over the back of his horse, in the direction of the rock formations in the distance. "Quiet, huh?" He pulled the saddle off the horse.

"You got a couple wagons full of immigrants down by the river. By where it forks," told Drummel. "They're in that area the Cheyenne used to hit, back in the day. What's it called?"

Corporal Miller Welch heard the sergeant's conversation. "Death Hollow. That's what the Pawnee call it."

"Death Hollow," whispered Wyllyams.

~

"Back again, Grimes?" asked Sergeant Mills.

None of the other soldiers seemed to notice, or care that Grimes had returned to the wagon. No one wanted to be chosen to relieve him.

"Sergeant, something's wrong with the herd. They're uneasy, not right. I know when livestock are trying to tell me something," Grimes said.

"Just how the hell do you know?" he asked.

"I watched over livestock, sheep to be exact, on our farm, back in Ireland," explained Grimes.

"I see. Well, you're not in Ireland anymore and those sure in the hell aren't sheep, are they?" Mills snapped. "Get what it is you came back for, then get back out there. Going to be time to head back soon."

"But sergeant, I---"

Mills stood, cutting him off. "Get your ass back out there, or else."

With nothing to do, but follow orders, Grimes turned back for the meadow. When he ascended the hill and laid his eyes back on the herd, all appeared calm. The usual noises a herd of cattle makes greeted him the closer he got. Where the meadow ended and the prairie took over, Private Eustice Clarence came into view.

"Clarence, I haven't seen you in some time."

Private Clarence didn't respond.

One arrow, then a second, whistled through the air and landed close to Grimes. His heart stopped, then burst into a rapid beat. He dropped to his knee. *Bang.* The shot did nothing to stop the mounted Indian warriors as they circled the herd. Clarence stumbled his way, his pace slow.

"Jesus Christ, get down and fire on them!" hollered Grimes.

No words answered his cry. Clarence stopped and collapsed, two arrows protruding from his back. Grimes picked up his rifle. *Bang.*

~

Keogh was uneasy and on edge for most of the day at the news of Custer attacking the Cheyenne. It caused him to wonder if the daily protocols in place throughout and around the fort for security were enough. Consumed with paperwork assigned to a post commander, he had struggled to get most of it done. It was useless he figured to try to force himself to do more, his concentration was gone. Besides, it was time for his afternoon rounds.

Before he entered the Adjutant's office, Keogh noticed a dust cloud to the west of the fort. For a moment, he thought nothing of it, until he scanned the surrounding prairie.

Nothing else moving. The herd!

He burst through the door, "Get me the officer of the day, now! Then find Comstock."

Clarke bounded out the door in search of the scout and the

duty officer.

"Nowlan, we getting any reports of Indian activity, coming across the wire?" asked Keogh.

Comstock flung open the door. "Rider just came in. Indians trying to run off all the livestock!"

The group bolted out the door to the parade grounds.

"Clarke, sound the alarm! All infantry out. Put out word to get all patrols back to the fort," ordered Keogh. "Then get G and I companies ready to move out. Have Mary Jo saddled for me. Nowlan, send out a wire."

The huge bell outside the Adjutant's office rang repeatedly, echoing over the prairie. Trumpeter Clarke had blown the alarm, followed by the commands, and the fort went into action.

Horse troopers ran to the stables to saddle their mounts. Infantrymen lined up in formation, then moved to their assigned areas for defense of the fort. Artillery crews moved cannons about the grounds and prepared them in case of an attack.

Keogh raced to the stables. Two companies of the Seventh Cavalry waited on him. Comstock and twenty Pawnee scouts were nearby, the scouts singing a song.

"What are they singing, Will?" Keogh asked.

"Giving one another courage," he explained.

Lieutenant Beecher pulled his horse alongside them. "All ready for duty, captain."

Keogh took the reins to Mary Jo from his orderly. "Easy, girl. Nothing to worry about." Keogh was concerned though. He had not had the time to get his new horse broken in for chasing Indians. Mary Jo was going to have to fight Indians one more time. Her eyes were big and soft. She and the other horses could sense the excitement and nervous energy from the troopers. He pulled himself onto the horse and shouted, "Mount up."

With his squad ready to leave, Sergeant Drummel mounted his horse. "So long, sergeant. See you back at Wallace in a few days."

The horses' ears rose and their heads angled toward the river. A faint muffled sound, floated across the prairie. A slight thumping, almost like...gunfire! No one moved.

Sergeant Wyllyams walked out to the edge of the station. Drummel dismounted and joined him.

"What do you suppose is going on?" Drummel asked.

"A raid. I'm sure of it."

"What now?"

"We get ready and sit tight."

"You don't think we should go to their aid?"

Wyllyams started back to the station. "That's what they want. They'll be here soon enough."

The Pawnee scouts led the horse troopers out. They had taken off their Army coats, preferring to ride into battle dressed in their traditional way of wearing only animal skins, their warrior charms and weapons.

The command, with Keogh in the lead, crested the hill. Below, the meadow opened to a chaotic scene. Infantrymen lined up together in a square formation, a wagon in the middle with the wounded in and around it. The soldiers fired on mounted warriors.

A Pawnee rode over to Comstock. The scout said something, then went back to the rest of his fellow warriors

"What did he say, Will?"

"Says they are Cheyenne."

Lieutenant Beecher had joined them. "Now what Keogh?" he

asked.

"You and Comstock take G Company---."

Before he could say more, the Pawnees let out a series of war cries. They charged on the Cheyennes. The herd moved towards the prairie.

"Got to go, Keogh. Now, Come on!" shouted Comstock.

"You two, don't let the men get away and run after them. You understand me? There's liable to more out there, just waiting for us to go charging!" Keogh shouted.

The two companies of cavalry advanced on the Cheyenne. The Pawnees already engaged, presented a problem. Amidst the fighting, the cavalrymen were unsure just who was friend and who was foe in this deadly contest of Plains Indian warfare. A challenge the Cheyenne used to their advantage. They drew the Pawnees close to the herd and to the cavalrymen. With their blood up and their horses hard to handle, the troopers let go shots that came closer to the scouts than the enemy.

With Trumpeter Clarke close, Keogh rode into the mix.

I can't even get a shot!

He pulled Mary Jo out of the oncoming herd's way, frustrated, but more alive than ever. To his right, two Pawnee drove a Cheyenne his way. "Come on, girl."

Mary Jo carried him into their path. With his revolver raised, he was ready.

Now, fire.

The oncoming Cheyenne ducked and slid to the side of his pony, passing Keogh, and unleashing an arrow at the trumpeter. Terrified, Keogh shouted, "Clarke!"

The Cheyenne's arrow was off target.

In the blink of an eye, the warrior wheeled his pony around toward Keogh. The warrior shot two arrows rapidly. Both just missed.

The Pawnees had come back around and intercepted the

Cheyenne. All three warriors' horses almost collided. *Bang.* The Pawnee's shot hit the Cheyenne.

Wounded, the Cheyenne turned and prepared another arrow.

Keogh felt as if his heart would burst from his chest. He raised his revolver.

He won't miss you again, hurry!

He steadied his hand and fired.

The scouts jumped off their horses. They sang and hollered as they scalped the Cheyenne, a scene Keogh and Clarke pulled away from.

Comstock rode in their direction. The Cheyennes were retreating. "It's over, Keogh!" he hollered, as he pulled up his horse alongside them.

"Sound recall, Clarke," ordered Keogh.

Night's coming on.

Nine
Death Hollow

Twenty soldiers waited. Their two sergeants, Wyllyams and Drummel, had positioned them throughout the station. As darkness closed in on soldiers and civilians, the prairie fell deathly quiet.

At the stable, the two sergeants met one last time to confirm their plan.

"I'll stay here," said Wyllyhams. "They'll come for the horses and stock first. Maybe we can scare them off?"

Drummel looked over the relay station, then cast his eyes in the direction of the river. "You think we did the right thing, sergeant?"

Wyllyams heard the true question hidden within his words. "I don't know what happened out there. All I know is night is about on us. Had we gone out there, who the hell knows what would have happened to us? This way, we got a good fighting chance here."

The two shook hands and moved to their men.

~

The fort was still on alert when Keogh and Comstock entered the grounds. As of yet, the only attack had been on the livestock. Night had settled in.

"We got lucky today," Comstock said. "If they'd gotten off with the herd, they would have tried the fort."

Keogh handed Mary Jo's reins to his orderly. "Clarke, pass the word. Officer's call at the Adjutant's office."

Lieutenant Nowlan poured himself a cup of coffee as Keogh and Comstock walked into the building. "I see you two survived. Want some?"

A nervous private moved from window to window, scanning

the prairie for any signs of movement.

"What's the latest?" Keogh asked.

"Nothing has come across the wire," responded Nowlan.

The officers trickled in, a few at a time. With reports given, the situation was stable.

"We will stay on full alert throughout the night. I want extra men around the stables," ordered Keogh.

Lieutenant Beecher came through the door. "Captain, Sergeant Drummel's squad has not reported back."

"Maybe they stopped short and holed up on account of Indians?" offered Captain Barnitz.

"I'll take a company out, captain," said Lieutenant Bell. "We'll find them. Drummel is a good man. Might have been forced to stay at one of the other stations."

"I'll go, too, captain," volunteered Lieutenant Cox.

All eyes were on Keogh. He stepped out onto the parade grounds and studied the dark prairie. The other officers followed him.

"No, we're staying put. Least until morning, that is," he finally said.

~

Shots echoed out of the darkness. Horses ran in circles, and the herd bellowed continuously. Sergeant Wyllyams had been right, the Indians moved for the animals first.

It was hard for the troopers to pick a target in the dark, and over animals as they moved about. Somehow, they landed a few close shots on the Indians attacking the stables and corral.

The attack stopped just as quickly as it had started. The prairie went eerily silent--- then a barrage of bullets riddled the station. Now, Indians moved for the station's living quarters, constant shots covering their advance. Those inside had been armed and ready. A hail storm of led greeted the attackers.

The Indians backed off to regroup, plotting where to next probe. Two simultaneous attacks enveloped the station, one again on the herd, the other--- this time more determined, hit the living quarters.

The cavalrymen were just as tough and hardened as the warriors who came at them. Violence met violence and those with shelter and extra ammunition held out.

With the sun coming up soon, the Indians headed off. They had wounded and what they took at Death Hollow to make off with. They'd need some time to distance themselves from the cavalry troopers, should they follow.

~

"Nothing better happen to this horse, you understand me?" snapped Keogh.

"I won't let nothing happen to her, captain. I promise," replied the trooper.

Keogh went to the head of the command where Comstock waited with ten Pawnee scouts. "Going to try your new horse out today?"

"I want to see how he does on a long march, that's all."

"You might get more than you bargained for on this one," Comstock said.

"Then I guess we shall see how he holds up. Command forward," ordered Keogh.

Sixty troopers from two companies of the Seventh Cavalry followed him from the fort. Every able body carried extra ammunition and extra rations. Pack animals with extra forage and more ammunition brought up the rear. A trooper pulled May Jo along. For the relay stations they went.

~

"Sergeant. Sergeant Wyllyams!" called Drummel.

Wyllyams pulled his horse through the scattered remains and debris of the campsite. Strewn throughout were clothes, broken furniture and four dead men. All four were full of arrows and scalped. Two dead women lay close. Their eyes, still open, told of the horror and tragedy.

"This women is still alive," said Drummel. "She looks to be pregnant, too."

She'd hid under a wagon. Her cries reached them, shock evident in her rambling. No one could understand her words.

Wyllyams listened closely. "Get Hageman over here."

Drummel gave the woman a drink from the canteen. "Easy, miss, easy." He looked at Wyllyams. "We got to get her to a doctor."

"Hageman, she sounds like she might be German," said Wyllyams. "See if you can make out what she's saying."

Private Hageman crawled underneath the wagon and knelt beside the woman. She cried and shook, but he grabbed her hand and spoke to her in German. She opened her eyes. Full of fear and terror, but now with some hope. She spoke back to the private, calm at first, but lapsing back into tears as she finished.

Hageman crawled back to join the men. "She says they were camped here when the attacked commenced. Said it happened so fast, they didn't have a chance. Those men are her husband, brothers and uncle."

The two sergeants looked at one another.

"There's more," said Hageman. "There were three young girls and her sister." His eyes lowered to stare at the ground. He looked up and pointed out to the prairie. "The Indians got them now!"

"Fix a travois for her," ordered Wyllyams. "Corporal Welch, take fiver troopers and this woman back to the station. Let them

60

know she's about to have a baby. Keep four men there to protect the place and her. God knows she has been through enough. You and one trooper then move back on the trail. Get to Chalk Bluff and Downer's Creek. Let them know what happened. From there, move on to the fort and let the captain know."

"What about us?" asked Drummel.

"The rest of you, prepare to move out. Hageman, tell her we're going after her family."

~

"How's your new horse?" Comstock asked as he pulled up by Keogh. "No signs of any war parties yet."

The day had turned hot. Keogh knew that since they'd passed Chalk Bluff Station, they would eventually turn away from the river if they had to move on to Monument Rocks Station. "Command halt. Dismount," he ordered. "Lieutenant Bell, pickets out. Lieutenant Cox, water the horses. One company at a time."

"You have learned well, Keogh," Comstock said, sliding off his horse. Lieutenant Beecher trotted up to them. With him came Fighting Bear, a Pawnee. Comstock spoke to the Indian scout. "Says Sky Chief and the rest moved on ahead to Death Hollow. Says something happened there."

With his command watered and ready, Keogh moved them on. His mind raced, he hoped Drummel and the others would be found alive at Monument Rocks Station. "Beecher, who replaced Drummel?"

"Sergeant Wyllyams, captain."

"There you have it," Comstock said. "None other than the sergeant himself, huh. Yes, sir, Keogh my friend. I told you, might get more than you bargained for on this one." He nudged his horse into a trot for the stand of trees close to the river called Death Hollow.

Under a patch of cottonwoods, set back from the river, the Pawnee scouts and Comstock dismounted. When Keogh, Beecher and Trumpeter Clarke arrived, six fresh graves greeted them, each with a wood cross pierced into the Kansas soil.

"Captain. Captain Keogh!" shouted Corporal Welch. He and a trooper accompanying him rushed past the dismounted companies.

Keogh was relieved when he heard troopers, but his joy was tempered when he saw only the two.

"Captain, we spotted you from afar, a ways back. We thought the scouts might be Cheyenne or Sioux, so we hid for a spell."

"What happened here?" Keogh asked.

"Indians hit a family of German immigrants before sunset last night. Then they came for us at the station," said Welch. "We managed to fight them off."

"Are Wyllyams and Drummel back at the station?"

"No captain. We found one pregnant woman still alive here. She told us Indians made off with three girls and one women," Welch told. "Sergeant Wyllyams sent me and five troopers with her back to the station. Then they lit out on their trail."

"Clarke, bring up Mary Jo. Prepare to move out," Keogh ordered.

Welch stayed by the graves and continued to look on. "Sergeant Wyllyams made sure we buried them, captain. Said it was bad enough he didn't come to help them last night."

Keogh looked at the graves, then at Comstock. "You got anything you want to say about Sergeant Wyllyams, now?"

Ten
Monument Rocks

"They are up yonder a ways, Sergeant Wyllyams," said the trooper. "Getting close to where all those rocks are. Sergeant Drummel says to come on ahead but be quiet about it. He and the others are in the timber."

Wyllyams turned to the men riding with him and gave the hand signal. The troopers dismounted and pulled their horses for the timber. As they neared the grove, Drummel waved them over.

"What's going on ahead?" Wyllyams asked.

"Looks like the girls are giving them trouble," said Drummel. "Might be some disagreement over something? They got some wounded, too. Here, take a look."

Sergeant Wyllyams and Drummel's men remained still, concealed in the timber. In the distance, they could hear the little girls' cries.

Wyllyams raised the field glasses to his eyes and searched the terrain. For whatever reasons, the Indians had stopped before entering the shelter of the rock formations. They were exposed and in the open. He scanned the war party. "Let's move on them while they're occupied."

"How many you figure?" asked Drummel.

"Enough to go around," Wyllyams told.

"What's your plan?"

"You take your squad to the right. We will go to the left," he said. "It's now or never. Night's coming on. We won't get a chance like this again."

"They might just go on and kill them when they see us," warned Drummel.

"What would you want if you were those children's parents?" Wyllyams asked. "For us to try, or for them to be taken, sold off and then only God will ever know what becomes of them."

~

Comstock and the Pawnee resumed tracking from Monument Rocks Station, ahead of the others. Keogh led the two companies after the scouts a short time later.

The trail the Pawnees followed told the story. Wyllyams and Drummel's party of cavalry troopers hunted an Indian war party.

To a grove of timber, smack in the middle of the prairie, the trail stopped. Ahead, another grove sat closer to the rock formations. Comstock and the scouts moved for the timber to wait for Keogh.

A dry Plains wind swept across the prairie, stinging man and horse. Keogh dismounted his command to cut down on the dust when he saw the Pawnee. The scout had come for them.

Short of the timber they stopped. Still dismounted, the troopers did their best to keep the horses quiet. Comstock came to the edge of the grove and waved them in, one company at a time.

With both his companies in the timber and in position to cover Comstock, Keogh raised his field glasses. The wind howled ominously against the stillness of the prairie. Muffled voices seemed to whisper around them, but the prairie revealed nothing to Keogh's eyes. Comstock and the Pawnee crept to the edge of the timber and were set to move for the next grove.

Suddenly, the roar of gunfire bounded across the prairie. All watched as two lines of blue clad horsemen charged out of the timber closet to the rock formations.

~

Wyllyams and Drummel had taken the Indian party by surprise, but it wasn't enough. At the outset of the firing, the captives had been thrown onto horses and pulled into the rock formations. The remaining warriors mounted their ponies and charged the cavalrymen. They were followed by another group of mounted warriors, previously hidden from sight within the rocks.

"Let's go. Move for the timber ahead!" ordered Keogh.

Out on the Kansas prairie, the two sergeants and fourteen troopers were engulfed by the warriors. The cavalrymen were courageous, but no equals when fighting from a horse. The Indians swirled around them.

Wyllyams took an arrow leading the attack, but somehow managed to stay on his horse. Fear, then a sense of helplessness gripped Keogh as he watched the warriors split up and attack the troopers.

The Indians rode close to the cavalrymen, unleashing arrows from behind their pony's neck. Before the troopers could fire a shot, the warriors would pull away, daring the cavalrymen to chase. Wyllyams wasn't able to keep his men in formation. Three troopers were killed in fierce fighting, but not before shooting down two Indians and unhorsing two more.

On the other side, Drummel fared even worse. Four troopers fell early in the fight. The remaining three were in a no man's land.

Rage surged through Keogh as he witnessed Wyllyams and Drummel's detail being destroyed. He had seen all he could take. "Beecher, you and Bell wait until we engage. Then move on those in the rocks. I Company, forward. Clarke, sound recall for those men."

I Company followed the Pawnee into the fight. G Company waited, then thundered out of the timber for the rock formations.

Dust clouded thick in the air, obscuring faces, removing the certainty of who was friend or enemy. Bullets flew and kicked up the ground. Comstock and the Pawnee were engaged ahead. Keogh saw an opening in the mix of fighters and spurred Mary Jo through it.

Suddenly, he flew over the horse's head as she toppled. Mary Jo staggered as she tried to get up. Then she lay back down.

Dazed, Keogh pulled himself to his feet and stumbled to his horse, not comprehending G Company retreating from the hail of gunfire from within the rocks.

Lieutenant Cox dismounted I company into a skirmish line. Their fire drove off the approaching warriors. "What now, captain?" he hollered.

Worried about Mary Jo, Keogh lost track of the action. Seeing the attack stopped, he did the only thing he could at the time. "Sound recall. Back to the timber. Please get up, girl, please!"

Comstock and the Pawnee dismounted by his side. G Company moved past and back for the timber with I Company covering the retreat. The warriors disengaged and moved for the safety of the rock formations.

Mary Jo screamed in pain as Sky Chief, the leader of the Pawnee, studied her front left leg. It was shattered from a bullet. The horse labored to breathe.

Panic and a sense of helplessness overcame Keogh. He looked ahead at the prairie, strewn with dead troopers. The Indians had returned, hacking and dismembering the dead. Others attempted to load their dead onto horses. "Fire on them, Goddammit! Those are our men out there! What the hell are you waiting for?" he shouted.

"I Company, back on skirmish line," ordered Cox. "Fire!"

Keogh backed away from his horse and squeezed his fist in rage. His beloved Mary Jo was dying right before his eyes. He knocked off his hat, running his hands over his head. He found it hard to breathe.

"Easy Keogh, easy," said Comstock. "We will help you."

Two other Pawnees, Fighting Bear and Blue Hawk, had dismounted. Together with Sky Chief, the three knelt around Mary Jo. They chanted and sang to ease her suffering. Each took turns stroking her. Sky Chief told her she would soon be in a better place.

His revolver in hand, Comstock cocked the hammer and walked up to the horse. The Pawnees backed away.

"No, wait," said Keogh. "She's mine." He knelt beside Mary Jo. Her eyes met his. She was scared. "I am so sorry. So sorry girl. Good-bye." He stood back up and pulled his revolver from the holster.

The shot rang out across the prairie. Keogh fell to his knees. More pain than he had ever known, or thought he could ever experience in his life, erupted and rushed over him.

You are their captain. Get up and get moving.

Myles Keogh brushed his hand over Mary Jo's head and neck. Slowly, his raised himself to his feet and picked up his hat. He looked at Mary Jo one last time, then turned and walked back to the timber without saying a word.

~

"We got them surrounded, captain," said Beecher. "All sides covered."

Keogh continued to stare at the trees, lost in thoughts of all those taken from him since coming to America. For a brief moment, he thought of Nelly.

"I got an idea," said Comstock. He squatted next to the small fire. "Night coming on. We might be able barter with them?"

"What in the hell are we going to give them?" Beecher asked.

"Their lives for the girls, that's what," said Comstock. He walked to the edge of the timber. The others followed. "We got them surrounded and outnumbered. Besides, they got wounded. Let them take their dead and loot, be gone."

"I want them dead!" Keogh said.

"That's just your anger talking. Use your head. Ain't no way for us to kill all of them before they kill those girls," said Comstock.

Keogh walked back to the fire. He looked at the assembled

group. "What's your plan?"

"I will go in under a white flag," Comstock said. "I will reason with them."

"Captain, permission to go around, to the men on the north," asked Beecher. "We got no officers there."

"Granted. What do you think about dividing the Pawnees up? Give each unit a couple," Keogh suggested.

"Now your back," Comstock smiled and relayed the plan to Sky Chief.

The Pawnee nodded his approval.

~

It was time. Comstock's horse trotted out ahead of Keogh and his troopers. The scout had fastened a white handkerchief to the end of his rifle. Keogh and Trumpeter Clarke rode close behind him, fifteen troopers and two Pawnee at their backs. When the other three units of cavalrymen saw the movement, they closed in.

The carnage from the fight greeted them the closer they moved to the rock formations. Mary Jo lay where she'd fallen. Keogh could hardly bear the thought of leaving her there, of her being picked apart by scavengers.

Some of the dead troopers had been stripped. Mitchell, Sergeant Wyllyams' horse, roamed close by. At the sight of the approaching troopers, he neighed and ran ahead, but stopped at the sound of his name being called. As they drew closer, a trooper grabbed his reins and pulled him along.

The body of Wyllyams lay closest to the rocks. He had been stripped, his body shot full of arrows. Both thighs displayed slash marks. His head had almost been completely decapitated from his torso, his right arm cut down to the bone.

"See those slash marks?" said Comstock. "That's a Sioux mark. Might be Brule or Oglala. The cutting of the arm could be a

Cheyenne mark."

"Can you speak any of those languages?" Keogh asked.

"Nope."

His new horse raised its head, ears at attention. His nostrils quivered toward the rock formations. Four mounted warriors appeared through an opening on the right side. On the far left, two others covered them.

"Stop them here," Comstock said.

Keogh signaled a halt. He, Comstock, and the trumpeter moved ahead, as did the four warriors. Twenty yards apart, both parties stopped.

Comstock did his best to communicate through sign language.

The warriors were Cheyenne, and a few Sioux rode with them. They wished to take their wounded and go home. Keogh watched the flurry of gestures. He thought he knew some of what was said but couldn't follow the speedy dialogue.

Comstock stopped signing. "They want to know what you will do, should they refuse to give up the woman and the girls?"

Keogh nudged his horse beside Comstock. "Tell them I only want the girls and the woman now. Let them know they can take their wounded and dead and go on." He glanced at both sides of the rock formations. In line, troopers and Pawnee scouts waited. "Let them know they will not leave here with the woman and girls, without us killing many of them."

A warrior's pony trotted a few steps closer, ahead of the others. The warrior signed to Comstock as he stared at Keogh. Comstock nodded his head. The warrior jerked on the pony's reins and the animal stepped backward, to join the others.

"He will let the girls and woman go," Comstock said. "Wants me to ride in with them. That way, after you get the girls and woman, you won't come on and attack."

"No way in hell, Will," said Keogh.

As he still faced the warriors, Comstock nodded. The warriors pulled away and galloped for the rocks. Comstock followed.

"Will. Damnit, Comstock! Wait!" Keogh shouted.

~

The silence grinded on Keogh. After a few agonizing minutes underneath the blazing sun, he dismounted. He moved ahead on foot, scanning the rock formations with his field glasses.

They're keeping us out here in the heat on purpose. Stupid, stupid, you are for letting Comstock go. You got no play now.

Then he saw the girl, and for a brief moment there was some relief for his worries.

She appeared in the opening crying, stumbling across the prairie towards Keogh and his men. Once she made them, the second began the journey.

After the third girl made it out, Comstock stepped from the opening to the rock formations, accompanied by the woman and two warriors.

"Welch, when the woman gets here, take two troopers and the girls into the timber. If something should happen, ride hard for the station," ordered Keogh.

"Will do, captain."

Comstock smiled and raised his hand.

Uneasy, Keogh looked on. His horse stepped sideways and jerked his head up and down. "Easy, you."

Is he telling me something?

In one fluid movement, a warrior pulled out a knife and drove it into Comstock's back. The woman screamed as the other Indian grabbed her by her wrist.

Comstock fell to the ground.

"Welch, get them out of here, now! Clarke, sound the charge!" shouted Keogh.

At the command, the other three units converged. Keogh's

70

horse bolted for the rocks.

Comstock pulled his revolver, targeting the warriors now distracted as their prisoner fought back. He managed to squeeze off four shots. Both warriors were dead before they hit the ground. The woman ran to him.

The cavalry troopers charged into the rock formations. The warrior's gunfire and arrows fell upon them. From the backside, Beecher's group entered. Keogh thundered past Comstock.

In the middle of the rock formations, the terrain split wide. Warriors charged about on ponies, others on foot darted for rocks. Those warriors wounded in the previous fight were cut down first.

There was no way for the cavalrymen to keep together. The units split off as the warriors scattered. Gunshots rang out, reverberating off the rocks. The warriors were trapped, though still fighting bravely.

A warrior ran to a huge piece of broken rock, jumped behind it and fired point blank on a pursuing trooper. The shot dropped the trooper from the saddle.

A Pawnee leapt from his horse onto a mounted Sioux. Both tumbled to the ground in a mix of dust and rocks. Each grabbed their knife. Sky Chief ran his pony into the Sioux. His fellow warrior pounced and drove his knife into the Sioux's chest.

Keogh chased a Cheyenne, his horse closing the distance rapidly. A shot nicked the animal's front left leg and he cantered sideways, then reared on his hind legs. When the horse landed, the warrior had turned, gun aimed.

Bang. The warrior missed. *Bang.* Keogh missed.

Before Keogh could fire again, the warrior pulled him from the horse.

The revolver flew from his hand. Keogh reached for another on the backside of his belt. He pulled it and cocked the hammer just as a mounted warrior charged him.

Out of the dust Keogh's horse ran at the pony. The two horses collided, sending the warrior flying into Keogh.

Flipping onto his stomach, Keogh half-raised himself from the ground, taking careful aim. In seconds, both warriors lay motionless. To his right, Keogh could see his horse as it pushed itself to its feet.

The horse just saved you.

Keogh reached for the horse, then blacked out.

~

They buried Sergeant Wyllyams at the edge of the timber where he'd led the charge, along with Sergeant Drummel and seven troopers. Next to this group, still under the timber's shade, Keogh's men buried six other Seventh Cavalry troopers.

And lastly, Will Comstock was laid to rest there as well.

The last grave dug was the biggest. Keogh's men had pulled Mary Jo off the prairie. She deserved to be honored with the rest.

The command was set to head back to Monument Rocks Station. Keogh was the last to leave the graves. The three lieutenants and the I Company farrier waited for him.

"Your horse will be fine, captain," said the farrier. "I cleaned and bandaged the wound."

Keogh took one last look at the graves. "All the girls and the woman mounted?"

"Yes, captain. All are ready," Beecher said. "Captain, I forgot to tell you something. Just came to me. We told Comstock what happened to you, with your horse and all. He just smiled and said to tell you, the two of you fought like Comanches."

Eleven
December 1868

Winter had come to the Plains. The cold crept in beneath the door and frosted the windows to Keogh's quarters. He knocked back a long drink of whiskey from his cup. Uneasy and depressed, he sat at the table and tried to read. How he wished he had some-one to talk to.

The months following the fight at Monument Rocks had been hard on Keogh. At times being able to concentrate was a challenge and the nightmares constant. Sometimes, they centered on the fight itself, others dealt with the war.

To make matters worse, all of those he had been close to at Fort Wallace were gone. Comstock was dead, and he could not forget the loss of Mary Jo. Back in the fall, Lieutenant Beecher was killed fighting Indians in the Colorado Territory. Nowlan had been sent with the rest of the Seventh Cavalry to the Indian Territory for a winter campaign.

Still in command of the fort, Keogh waited to rejoin the Seventh until his replacement arrived. He received the report of the Seventh's fight with Indians on the Washita River the same time his orders to report to the Indian Territory came through. The story ran in all the major newspapers across the country. The Seventh Cavalry was famous, but there he sat, idle and out of the action.

Major Elliot was on the casualty list as well. The loss of another friend and the thought of how he'd missed out on a chance for some glory, something to justify his time in the Army, only added to his misery. Keogh thought of Nelly often. She still had not returned a single letter. Never in his life had he felt so lonely.

Twelve
February 1869
Camp Supply

"Well, look who it is, boys?" Captain Benteen called out. "He finally got himself free to chase some Indians again."

Keogh had rejoined the Seventh in the Indian Territory.

He smiled at the sight he found. Most of the regiment's officers spending the cold night around a huge fire.

"You know you're my favorite Irishman, Keogh," Benteen laughed. A hardy roar rose among the officers present. Benteen grabbed an empty cup. In one swift motion, he filled it with whiskey and handed it to Keogh. "Sit down and join us. You can rest as we tell you how we've spent a wonderful winter out here on the Plains."

"I read the reports and the newspapers. The more I saw, the more eager I was to be out there with you all," said Keogh.

Silence fell over the group. Most drank quietly and stared at the fire.

"Don't believe everything you read in the papers, Keogh," Benteen said, his jolly tone turning suddenly dark.

The tension was easy to feel. But Keogh needed to know. "Alright, tell me how Elliot got himself killed."

"When you go charging into an Indian village, there's going to be casualties," Benteen said. The captain stared into the fire, swigging his whiskey. Then he looked up, right into Keogh's eyes. "I'll tell you with every honest bone in my body, Keogh, that son-of-a-bitch Custer left Elliot and those men out there."

"Go on."

"Smith was sent down the river and looked for Elliot and his men. For whatever reason, he came back without finding them," said Benteen. "I was told some of Elliot's own company joined the search, but who knows whether they could not hear them fighting over of our dear commander's love of shooting horses and dogs for entertainment?"

Keogh was speechless. He scanned the men's faces. Not a word was spoken by any. "If you had the village under control, why did you pull out before Elliot was found?"

"Ah, yes. It don't add up, does it, Keogh?" Benteen said. He stood, his eyes filled with anger. "I'll tell you why. It's because that dumb bastard Custer didn't have any idea just how big of a damn village we were hitting. He kept us there, burning and tearing down a bunch of tipis. We had to gather the women and children, too, and there he was, like I told you, shooting Indian ponies and dogs. All that time, nobody looking for Elliot, and what do you know? We almost get ourselves surrounded by Indians coming from down the river Custer hadn't thought to scout! For God's sake, man! We found Elliot and his men two weeks later, frozen and mutilated beyond anything imaginable. Their wives wouldn't even have recognized them!"

"Elliot took off on his own! He shouldn't have gone so far away from the regiment. We know it, and so do you, Benteen," someone argued from across the fire.

Benteen wheeled away from Keogh, threw his cup into the fire, and confronted the voice. "You goddamn stupid sons of bitches!" He glared at the faces before him. "You think that maniac cares about any of us? Remember what Elliot looked like when we found him? That's what will happen to each of us. Maybe not now, but mark my words! Custer's going to get us all killed, if we're not careful! For what, I wonder? So he can get another medal to put on his chest and write some damn book about it!"

Enough had been said for now. Benteen returned to his stump and slumped his tired body onto it. Slowly, the others rose and headed back to their tents.

Only Keogh and Benteen remained. Embers popped and

cracked, sending sparks into the air. Keogh studied Benteen's face. It was weathered, defined by his time on the Plains. The stress of a military life had begun to leave marks on the captain.

"What will you do, Benteen?"

The captain just stared into the fire. He closed his eyes and raised his chin to the sky. "Keogh, my wife just lost our baby girl, little Kate." He looked up at the stars. "Do you know Custer is sending me to Fort Dodge while the rest of you all go to Fort Hays? That place is so awful. I'm sending my wife back to St. Louis."

Keogh rose from his stump and walked over to Benteen. He placed his hand on the captain's shoulder. "I am truly sorry for you and your wife's loss. What are you planning to do about Custer?"

"It's already done."

"What in the hell do you mean?"

"I have friends who know people, Keogh. I wrote them a little story. I'm sure the American people will be interested to learn that, while the great boy general was shooting horses and dogs, his men were fighting for their very lives. All the while, he never sent out a search party. He didn't give a shit."

"What are you going to do when he finds out?"

"Let him try something with me. He don't have the guts!"

~

Given new orders, Keogh prepared to leave the Indian Territory. He had been reassigned to duty inspecting Army forts throughout the southwestern United States. It was not what he'd had in mind when he rejoined the Seventh, but orders were orders. Besides, he'd been in no hurry to return to Kansas. The rest of the Seventh waited to move on to Fort Hays.

A trumpeter blew the command.

Keogh stopped the packing of his gear.

Officers' call, now?

He listened to the raised voices nearby.

"What in the hell is he doing blowing an officers' call at this time of the day?"

"He probably has more rules and regulations he wants to tell us all about," said another officer.

The Seventh Cavalry's officers lined up and stood at attention for the briefing. Their commander, General George Custer appeared.

It was plain to see the general's anger and agitation. He quick--stepped to the men as though ready for a fight. Accompanying the general was his brother, Captain Tom Custer. The Regimental Adjutant, Lieutenant Cooke and the Sergeant Major followed.

When Keogh had joined the regiment, he'd met Tom and Cooke, the three of them becoming close and trusted friends. He could see both were nervous, their eye's darting back and forth from the men to the general.

"The reason I have sounded officers' call is simple," General Custer said. "It seems there is a traitor among us. Someone sent a false account of the happenings at the Washita to the newspapers back east."

The general's accusation met a stunned silence.

Keogh's heart pounded. Would Benteen do something rash?

The general walked up and down the line of officers. The whole time, he slapped his leg with a riding crop. "This gutless coward has not only insulted me and my reputation, he has insulted the entire regiment as well. I shall have him horse- whipped!" He wheeled to his left and turned from the officers.

Benteen looked to the right, then left. A moment later, he stepped forward, out of line.

Panic came over Keogh as he watched Benteen calmly unsnap his revolver holster. Next, the captain removed the revolver and cocked the hammer. He put the revolver back into its holster, the flap left unsnapped.

"It was I, General, who wrote the letter. I am none the worse for having done so," Benteen said.

General Custer spun around and faced the men. His eyes widened, filled with the shock of betrayal. The general and Benteen looked like two dogs, hackles raised, ready to square off.

"You, Benteen? I will see you again about this!" he shouted.

Benteen stared straight ahead. A smirk flashed across his face.

The general did nothing more, but turned and stomped away.

Not a man stirred or moved. Benteen walked away first.

~

Keogh entered his tent. He couldn't believe what he had just witnessed. He loosened his shirt collar and onto the cot he threw himself. Benteen and Custer's altercation had left him with a sense of uneasiness. Never, in Italy or the war, had he experienced such conduct. He closed his eyes and tried to sleep, but it was no use.

The drink of whiskey did nothing to calm his nerves. His thoughts turned to Nelly and Ireland.

Get out of this place. Get her and go home.

Sweat dripped down his forehead. He felt like a caged animal.

Maybe Benteen is right; Custer will get us killed.

Having cheated death for some time now, Keogh knew in his heart that it would catch up to him one day. Why it came to him now, he was not sure. He pulled himself from the cot and grabbed some paper and pencil. Keogh made up his mind then and there. He was going home.

Thirteen
1871
New York

Determined to continue on with his military career, Keogh prepared to return to the Army and the frontier. The trip home to Ireland had restored his spirit and determination. Still in good health, he just knew there were more opportunities if he stayed soldiering.

The Seventh Cavalry had new orders and, with them, a new destination. They were to be sent to the Dakota Territory, assigned with the task of subduing the Native American Plains Indians that had not submitted to government control and reported to the reservations. Myles Keogh would not miss a chance like this.

"You have a letter, Mr. Keogh," said the ship's clerk.

A single letter waited for him. The return address Auburn, New York.

Nelly?

Hesitant and scared of what the letter might say, he left the ship without opening it.

Probably telling me not to write her anymore. She's found another. Not some damn fool soldier.

Before he'd left for Ireland, he had written her a letter asking if she might meet him before he went home, apologizing for any pain he might have caused her. Nelly never came. Yet, this letter. His heart beat faster. He had to know.

Dearest Myles,

Please forgive me for not returning your letters. I know I have hurt you, my dear. You must understand this is not who I am, or who I want to be. I am still in love with you, and I wish I could be there to greet you when you return to the states. I am at Willowbrook, taking care of Emily. Consumption has finally won its battle with the poor girl. Oh, how I wish you were here to comfort me

81

and Upton. The past year has been so hard on the both of us. Please write or wire me when you return. I hold on with the hope of hearing from you.

Love,

Nelly

Lost in his thoughts, Keogh read the letter again. He thought for sure his mind had played some cruel joke on him.

She still loves me, after all this time.

It was all he needed.

~

Keogh read the letter over and over through the seemingly never-ending train ride to Auburn. It was early evening when he arrived at Willowbrook. He stood outside the mansion, beneath the trees, and looked around the estate. There was a certain type of serenity here. He closed his eyes and took a deep breath before summoning the courage to approach the front door. He waited for an answer to his knock, hoping it would be Nelly.

"Good evening, Captain Keogh. I wondered if we would ever see you again," said Jack Martin.

"It sure is good to see you, Jack. May I ask to come in, to visit with Nelly?"

Jack Martin was a younger brother to Nelly. He ushered Keogh into the house and took his bags, leading him to the kitchen before excusing himself to find Nelly.

As Keogh waited, he found his way to the wash room and studied his reflection in the mirror. He wished he looked better for her. With some clean water and soap, he washed his face, combed his hair and adjusted his uniform.

On his way back to the kitchen, he saw her. She was more

beautiful than he'd remembered. Time had not diminished anything about Nelly Martin. He hoped she would feel the same about him. As he walked up behind her, she turned.

"Myles Keogh," she said as she threw her arms around him.

Keogh closed his eyes. Everything in the world was right at that moment. They held each other. Over so many lonely nights on the plains he had waited to hold her. "My God, Nelly. If you only knew how I've thought about what I want to say."

"Let me see my soldier." She wiped away a tear.

"I thought I'd never see you again. How is Emily?"

"I'm afraid it's only a matter of time. Upton is here with her. He will be so glad to see you. He's taking it very hard, of course. We talk of you often and wonder what new adventure you are living."

"Nelly, I am so---"

She placed her finger against his lips and gently kissed his check. "We can talk and catch up later." She turned and led Keogh up to Emily's room.

From the door, they could see Emily asleep. Upton dozed in a chair beside her, and Keogh eyed the two of them. He noticed how they had aged.

Who would be by my bed if a similar fate should befall me?

The next couple of days went by quickly. Even with the tragic event of Emily's struggle casting a shadow over the entire family, Keogh still felt the love he'd found on his previous visits to Willowbrook.

Days were spent with Upton, reminiscing. "Is it like the papers say, Keogh? Is the West the strange and mysterious place it is made out to be?"

"It's a different world out there Upton, that is for sure. Why, there are times it seems like the prairie will go on forever. The weather can change in the blink of an eye."

"What about fighting the Indians, Keogh?"

"There's nothing romantic about it. Fighting Indians is a tough and brutal business. It's not like the war was."

Upton lowered his head in hands. After a short while he gazed up at Keogh. "Sometimes, I wonder what would have become of me, if I'd never met her, Keogh. I can't stand the thought of losing her, but I wonder if I missed out on seeing...well, you know."

"Upton, you have missed out on nothing. The Army is not like it was in the war. It is harsh and lonely. The Plains are no place for a family. You're the lucky one."

Afternoons found Keogh and Nelly taking long walks around the property. There was so much catching up to do.

Try as he may, Keogh never seemed to find the right time or words to tell Nelly his true feelings. After having not seen her in so long, and with Emily's condition, the time was not right; he could sense it. But he was torn. How could he ask about their future, with everything she had to endure? Or even mention to her he might stay on a little longer with the Seventh, as they went to the Dakota Territory. A part of him was relieved they never discussed the future now. He wanted to go out west. Sure that something great would happen in an Indian campaign.

~

The morning of his last day at Willowbrook, Keogh was awakened by the wonderful smell of fresh biscuits, eggs and coffee. Once downstairs, he was met by several of the family members he'd not seen since his return.

"Dear Lord, please, in this family's time of sorrow, let us not forget you are our savior. In your name, we give thanks for this food. Please keep our darling Emily in the palm of your hand, and we say thanks for bringing our good friend, Myles Keogh, back to us. In your name we pray, amen," said Mr. Martin.

Much of the conversation centered on Keogh's days in Kansas

and chasing Indians.

"Myles, tell us how accurate the newspapers are with the stories of the Indians?" pressed Mr. Martin.

"Indians are not the savages they are made out to be. An Indian warrior is trained from birth for warfare," Keogh said. "They are second to none when it comes to riding and fighting from a horse."

"What about the Seventh Cavalry?" Jack asked. "What's it like?"

Keogh listed the characters who made up the United States Seventh Cavalry's officers. "There is Captain, Tom Custer, the general's younger brother. He's a winner of two Medals of Honor. Another captain is George Yates, who served with General Custer in his Michigan Regiment, during the war. Captain Benteen is a soldier you'd want in a fight with you. I can't forget the lieutenants, either; Cooke from Canada, Nowlan from England, Mathey from France and DeRudio from Italy. All are Civil War veterans, master story-tellers, and men I not only consider fellow soldiers, but good friends."

Lieutenant DeRudio's story was a favorite of Keogh's. "DeRudio attended military school in Austria and fought in Italy. From there, he was in on a plot to kill Napoleon the Third. Having been found guilty of such doing, DeRudio was sentenced to Devil's Island, which he escaped and then made his way to America. Captain Benteen calls DeRudio Count No Account for his hearty story-telling."

After breakfast, when all goodbyes were said, Nelly took Keogh to meet his train. It reminded him of their last time together, how badly it had ended. He was determined this time to let no such thing happen. Yet, words still eluded him.

Nelly broke the silence. "Myles, thank you for the wonderful surprise visit. I can't think of a recent time when my family's spirits have been lifted so. Fate has put us here for a reason. That's good enough for me. I will wait for you. I now know I need you in my life. I'd hoped, by not talking to you, it would ease the memories. I know I cannot ask of you what you cannot do right now in your life." She pulled the wagon to a stop beside the train station.

It was his turn, suddenly the words were clear. Before he spoke, he reached into his travel bag and pulled out a photo. "Here, this is for you, to remember me." The photo was of him standing between two horses.

She studied the photo. "Are both of these horses yours?"

"Yes, I am lucky to have both. The one on my right is my good boy, Paddy. When I ride him out on the plains, it's as if he and I are riding the wind, Nelly."

She smiled and looked up at him. "What about this other one?"

"Well, that is a special horse. His name is Comanche. To tell you the truth, that horse is like no other I've ever had. Why, I tell you, he is so smart, Nelly, and he has a temper to go along with this---this incredible courage. I feel it from him. When we're out chasing Indians, he seems to sense them, has a nose for danger. There is something spiritual, too, about him. Yes, that's it. I feel safe. No matter the situation, he will get us out of it. He's my guardian angel. I shall bring both back with me when I return to stay." Keogh stopped himself as the last words flew out of his mouth. He'd said it, and she'd heard it. He could see the relief shining in her eyes. He would come back to Nelly.

~

The train ride back to Kansas to rejoin the Seventh Cavalry proved harder than Keogh could have ever imagined. At times, he desperately wanted the train to arrive, and other moments he wished only to get off and race back to Nelly. What stopped him, he couldn't figure.

He tried to sleep, but in his closed eyes danced the figures of his past that now seemed so long ago. Memories of the war haunt-

86

ed him.

When sleep did find him, a dream made a haunting reappearance. It started shortly after the war, and each time it came, it was the same. He walked past dead Union Soldiers as they lay waiting to be buried. As the dream continued, he would come to the realization that he was not walking, but being carried to join the ranks of the dead.

When Keogh woke from the nightmare, sweat soaked his uniform shirt, and he'd forgotten where he was. In need of some fresh air, he rose from his seat and made his way to the rear of the train. As he sat in the cold air, he tried to forget the horrible dream. He closed his eyes as the landscape flew by him.

If this train stopped now, I would grab the next one back to her.

The train didn't stop that night, and Myles Keogh didn't get off it when it did stop later that morning. Instead, he let it carry him back to Kansas and the Seventh Cavalry. He dismissed his bad dream.

You have to stay on for a little longer. Something good will happen out west. You will be part of it. It is your destiny.

Fourteen
1873
Dakota Territory

"Mail, we've got mail!" announced the sergeant.

It was the news that, when said, gave all men in any outfit an excuse to stop what they were doing. Sometimes, a single letter, was all that kept a man sane on the frontier. Keogh joined the hopefuls milling about the sergeant.

The resolve to embrace his military career and live a life away from Nelly had been tougher than expected. Once back on duty in the Seventh Cavalry, Keogh's mood had blackened. The past years had been a disappointment. In the Dakota Territory, he and his I Company had yet to be posted with the rest of the Seventh at Fort Lincoln.

Indecision became a daily struggle and constant part of his routine. He was away from the core of the Seventh's officers, the men who made the Army tolerable for him. He missed Nelly and the Martin family. The mundane daily duties of being an escort to surveyors depressed him and he longed for some type of action to set his soul free. Hope of one last defining moment, something to end his career with, had come and gone like a fleeting dream.

"Here is your mail, captain," I Company First Sergeant Frank Varden said.

"Thank you, First Sergeant," replied Keogh.

Three letters had come for him. One from his family in Ireland, one from Nelly, and one from Lieutenant Cooke.

Keogh and his Company I had been sent with Major Reno to the remote outpost of Fort Totten, Dakota Territory. Here, with Reno and Captain Weir and his D Company, the two companies guarded surveyors as they laid out the boundary between Canada and the United States. The post held no glory, no excitement.

Major Marcus Reno was a West Point graduate. The Seventh's second highest ranking officer, he should have been stationed with the regiment at Fort Lincoln. But bad blood between him and General Custer had kept the major away when at all possible.

Captain Thomas Weir came from Michigan and was a highly decorated Civil War veteran. A good leader of men, Weir was rumored to have caught the eye of the general's wife, another officer banished.

Any news from Cooke was welcomed, especially when it came to keeping Keogh updated on what was going on with the Seventh Cavalry. He'd begun to feel like he was being pushed out of General Custer's favored inner circle of officers. More than once, it had donned on him that he was stationed with two men who had earned the general's distaste; had he done something to earn a similar fate? He also dwelled on the knowledge that Benteen was stationed at Fort Rice, also separated from the regiment. He tried not to put too much stock into it, but his doubts were hard to shake.

Dear Keogh,

We just got back from a hot time of it up on the Yellowstone. You should have been there, my friend. We left Fort Lincoln to guard the Northern Pacific Railroad surveyors as they looked for a route through the Rockies. We ran into the Sioux on a couple of occasions. I tell you, Keogh, they don't seem to be too scared of us. They almost lured the general into a trap when he was scouting way out in front of us. A second time, they attacked our camp. Can you believe that? We skirmished with them, and it was a hot affair to boot. They scattered once we filled the air with some cannon shot! The general is not overly concerned with their ability or desire to organize and fight as a unified force. An Indian warrior seems more worried about personal bravery deeds than he does in the outcome of a battle.

We keep getting word that gold was discovered in the Black Hills. Don't know what we can do about it, but I heard we may take us a little trip into the hills to look for ourselves soon. Don't worry too much about not being here. I will do what I can to get you back with us.

Your friend,

W.W. Cooke

And so, the months passed and time went by ever so slowly for Keogh on the border. It was beautiful country, full of wild game. Most days were spent hunting once the surveying crew had completed their work. Nights, though, seemed to last forever, constant thoughts of Nelly haunting him. He'd found a bit of a reprieve in the company of Reno and Weir. If both were in good spirits, their stories from the war were as good as any who served.

~

"Telegram for you, Captain Keogh," said the operator at Fort Totten.

He knew who and where the telegram had come from. Keogh hoped it would bring him good luck. Was this the opportunity he had stayed in the Army for? He so desperately needed one last chance to prove he was a soldier again.

The telegram was from Cooke. The lieutenant said he and Tom Custer had gone to the general on Keogh's behalf in an effort to get him and his company back to Fort Lincoln. The general had contacted Army headquarters for the Dakota Territory to regain I Company, but it was to no avail. The orders were for Keogh and his company to stay put. He was to continue guarding the survey parties.

Cooke finished the telegram with more disappointing news. The Seventh Cavalry was headed into the Black Hills on a surveying expedition. For years, gold had been rumored to be abundant in the area. There was sure to be action, as the hills belonged to the

Sioux. Keogh would miss yet another chance for action.

Why stay now? I missed my moment again. I'm going home, to hell with all of them.

To leave behind the Dakotas and the Army was all Keogh could think of. If the general couldn't assign them to Fort Lincoln, then it was time to head back to Nelly. His furlough had been granted some time ago. He'd wanted to see Ireland again as well. Something nagged at him, a suspicion. Perhaps it was time to start making plans about his future.

Keogh sent Cooke a return telegram containing Nelly's address at Willowbrook. He told the lieutenant how he was off to Ireland and then to New York, and implored his friend to update him on the Black Hills expedition upon his return.

Fifteen
December 1874
Auburn, New York

He had made it back to her. Keogh was ready to leave the Army and share a life together with Nelly. When he arrived in Auburn this time, he knew he'd made her happy. She smiled constantly in his presence and when he'd look at her, she blushed.

Keogh imagined how this could be his life. Winter in western New York was at hand, bringing with it beauty that added to the appeal of making such a place his home. He and Nelly spent the days walking, lost in conversation. Other times, the two worked on odd jobs around Willbrook, and he loved it. For the first time since leaving home, he felt he belonged somewhere.

Evenings were spent with her family around the dinner table. Afterwards, he entertained all with stories of the Seventh Cavalry, the Dakota Territory and Indians. It was just like the first visits, complete and happy.

During the last week of his leave, Keogh received the letter he'd been waiting for. Hesitant to read it, he put it aside and tried to forget it was there.

Don't open it. Just throw it in the fire.

But he couldn't. Had the newspapers been true? He had to know what Cooke said about all the Seventh Cavalry had found in the Black Hills.

Dear Keogh,

Sending you this letter, as you asked. I am sure by now you have read about the Seventh's adventure into the Black Hills. They left Fort Lincoln in July with 1,000 men. With them went surveyors, miners, and geologists. They did find gold in those hills, Keogh! As we speak, the United States government is trying to buy the Black Hills from the Sioux. I doubt they sell. The Arikara scouts tell me the Black Hills are very sacred and spiritual to the Sioux. You know what that will mean.

The general says, sometime in the next year or so, the Seventh will be going out. The government has to send the Army to round up all the Indians we can, in an effort to settle the frontier once and for all. The general says it will take all of the Seventh together, along with other outfits in a massive campaign. Get back here soon. We will have the entire regiment together at Fort Lincoln.

Your friend,

W.W. Cooke

There it is.

His rendezvous with destiny was sure to happen; a chance at glory and fame was now within his reach. The uneasiness of having to tell Nelly settled into his stomach. He was glad he had not read the letter aloud to her.

Although Keogh wanted to walk away from the Army, a part of him, that inner voice who knew he had a chance at more, would not let him. There was no way he could. Myles Keogh had to have something big to end his career with. It was all there for the taking. He had to go.

Now, came the hard part.

Nelly. How will I convince her to hang on a little while longer?

~

"You have been rather quiet these last couple of days, Myles," said Nelly.

Keogh had hoped to avoid this kind of conversation. A sadness always found him on his last day with Nelly, made only worse as his mind raced to come up with a way to tell her about the letter. He purposely ignored her last comment as he packed his bags.

94

Just stop leaving her, you damn fool.

"Myles, is everything alright?"

"Yes. Nothing to worry about."

It was the best he could offer. Keogh wanted to get out of the bedroom and down the stairs to breakfast. The last thing he wanted to do was tell her he was staying on in the Army a little bit longer, so he could chase Indians.

Once downstairs, Nelly prepared the two of them breakfast. It was still too early for the rest of the family to be up. Keogh took his coffee to the front porch and Nelly followed, studying him for some time without his knowledge.

"How long have you been standing there?" Keogh asked as he finally spotted her.

"Long enough to see your worry."

"It's that obvious?"

"To me, it is. What's wrong?"

"Nothing really. A letter I received the other day. I'm afraid it is causing me to..." He couldn't even manage to look her in the eye.

Nelly sat in a rocking chair. She wiped away a tear with her apron. "I knew I couldn't make you stay. Father and my uncle had a conversation about gold being discovered in the Black Hills some time ago. The whole time they were talking, I was trying to think how I could keep you from going back out there."

"I just got to go back now, Nelly. Just for a little bit longer. Cooke says we'll be going out on a big Indian expedition." He knelt in front of her. "Why, once we round up all the Sioux and Cheyenne, the West will be tamed forever. Think about it. What stories and tales I can weave. With this little bit of fame, who knows where all of this can end up?"

"You're such a dreamer." She traced a finger down his jaw as she cried. She turned away, unable to look him in the eyes.

"What is it, Nelly? I know I've asked a great deal from you, but I promise, this is it. After all this business is said and done, I am

95

yours forever." Keogh took her hands and kissed them both.

"It's not the waiting for you, my dear. It's the waiting to hear that you won't be coming home at all!"

Her words hit him hard. For a moment, Keogh felt as if his heart had stopped. He rose and sat in the nearest chair, taking in all of her last words. "What do you mean by that?"

Nelly reached for his hand. "I hoped that, by keeping you with me, I wouldn't have to hear how you died out there on the Plains. I've always had a terrible premonition that something bad will happen to you out there. Ever since we first met back in Tennessee, I've felt it. You have been cheating death too long, Myles." She started to sob.

"Nelly, listen to me. I'm riding in the best outfit in the entire United States Army. Why, you think I'm some kind of hero? These other men put me to shame. If you only knew all they've done and the places they fought. Please don't worry about such things." He leaned over and gently kissed her cheek. "You forget I have a great horse. Remember Comanche? Why, he's so smart and has great instincts, Nelly. I feel like he can get me out of any situation."

"Good." She stood and wiped her eyes with her apron again. But there was more; Keogh could see it in the hard lines of her lips. "Myles, promise me something. I mean, you promise me this, right here and now."

"Anything, Nelly. Anything."

"If you ever find yourself in a bad way out there--- and I mean so bad that, no matter how hard you try, it's not going to work--- you let Comanche carry you away and don't look back. Don't you look back! Just the two of you run back here to me. Don't you try to save all of them from going to hell, you hear me? You have nothing to prove to any man, Myles Keogh. You have fought and done enough in your lifetime. Your soul needs to rest. Please, Myles, please!"

The anxiety and apprehension from waiting on him all those

years burst through. Nelly collapsed into gasps and sobs, her shoulders shaking. She moved away from Keogh, leaning on a porch step column.

Keogh mulled over her request. She was asking him to save himself--- if it came to that out there. He stepped to her side and pulled her against him. "I promise you, Nelly Martin. I promise you now, and I promise I will love you forever. I promise, I will come back to you." Into her hand, he slid his last medal from the Pope.

Part Two

One
March 1876
Fort Abraham Lincoln
Dakota Territory

While he waited to meet his fellow soldiers, Keogh read the maps in the officers' club room. He focused on the topography of the Dakota and Montana Territories. The Seventh Cavalry had been rumored for some time to be going on a campaign that could take them through the western part of the Dakota Territory and possibly into the Montana Territory. The task would be to find the last hostile Native American Indians holding onto their old ways of roaming the plains, hunting buffalo and waring on other tribes. The Seventh would then use force, if needed, to drive the Indians to the reservations. Keogh was lost in thoughts of just how big and vast a territory the Seventh was expected to cover.

"Keogh, there you are," said Lieutenant Charles DeRudio.

"You're a damn sight for sore eyes, old friend!" called out Henry Nowlan. The lieutenant had served under Keogh in Kansas and was now the Seventh Cavalry's Quartermaster. First Lieutenant Edward Mathey followed.

"Well, if it isn't the French Foreign Legion's cast offs in my midst," Keogh said.

"How are you, Keogh?" asked DeRudio.

"I'm good. Glad to be back in the company of friends."

"Let's get a whiskey and catch up on old times," said Nowlan.

A bottle was ordered and at a table the four sat. Keogh had not seen the three in over two years. There was much to discuss, especially with all the news circulating on post regarding the regiment getting word when they might leave on campaign.

"So, what have you three heard? Are we going out for sure?"

asked Keogh.

"We don't know anything, nor are we ever told any news until we're in it," replied Nowlan.

"You know more than all of us put together, Keogh," Mathey said.

"That's right," said DeRudio. "You forget, we're not friends of Tom Custer like you."

"DeRudio, you've forgotten that I'm just like you. A foreigner in this man's army," Keogh said.

"No, you're not like us," told Nowlan. "You travel through all the circles in this regiment."

A group that included Captains Tom Custer, Yates, Weir and Myles Moylan, along with Lieutenant Cooke and Lieutenant James Calhoun entered the room.

The mood inside the club was a festive one, with Keogh at the center of most conversations. For the first time in a long time, he felt at home with the regiment. The atmosphere quickly shifted when Major Reno walked through the door. Reno did not have many friends in the regiment.

"Christ almighty," groused Weir. "I can't go nowhere, it seems, without having to see that man."

"Oh, for God's sake, Weir," Yates said. "It's just Reno. Everyone knows he's full of himself."

Moylan nodded. "We all know how hard it can be to deal with him, but it's not like the man is Napoleon, is he now, DeRudio?"

A hearty laugh went up among all sitting close. DeRudio's story-telling of his days as a soldier in Europe were of legendary proportions.

"You all haven't had the pleasure like Captain Keogh and I have had over the last couple of years, of being exiled with the major," Weir pointed out. "The major is convinced the general doesn't like him."

A quiet hush settled over the group as Reno moved toward

them.

"Don't stop on my account men. Go on with your story, Keogh. I'm sure I've heard it already, but they never get old," he said.

Try as he might, Reno never seemed to say the right words. The major and a Lieutenant Hodgson moved to a table by themselves, leaving the group quiet for a moment.

"What's the latest news about us going out after the Sioux, Cooke?" asked Moylan.

"The general hasn't said too much, other than it will only be a matter of time," replied Cooke. "He said it's got to happen soon. Washington wants to open up the Black Hills."

"It'll make me feel a whole lot better when we get the regiment together so we can do some training," added Yates. "It's sure good to have you back with us, Keogh. Why, I even wish Benteen was here. If we're to go out after all the hostiles, we need officers with Indian fighting experience."

"Hell, Yates, nobody cares about that damn Benteen," Moylan said.

"You should care about Benteen," Yates argued.

"And why in the hell should I care about Benteen?" asked Moylan, rolling his eyes at the captain. "He don't like no one here, except Keogh."

"We need Benteen and his fighting experience. We don't have that many men or even that much experience among us here when it comes to fighting Indians," Cooke said. "We've never even had all twelve companies together before, let alone fighting together."

"I wouldn't get too concerned with the Indians out here and their fighting abilities, Cooke," remarked Lieutenant Algernon Smith, who had joined the group unannounced. "We didn't have too much trouble with them on the Yellowstone. Hell, we didn't even see any on our expedition into the Black Hills."

"Really, Smith?" asked Cooke. "Shows what you know. Ask

Tom and the others here about what almost happened to the general up on the Yellowstone. You think the Sioux only fight through ambush or better numbers? Well, you're wrong."

"Cooke's right," said Yates. "The general has gotten us into some situations where we were lucky as hell to have made it through."

"How are the regiment's NCOs?" asked Keogh. He knew the backbone and strength to any outfit rested in the non-commissioned officers.

"Strong and seasoned," replied Cooke. "We got one hundred and fifty new recruits back in October. It's anybody's guess if they've had any previous military experience. In this outfit, you never know if an enlisted man is who he says he is."

"There are many questionable characters among us," said Weir. "Many of these recruits barely know how to ride a horse."

"I got the most new recruits out of any of you," Tom said.

"You are a fine one to talk," said Moylan. "Why, you might have the strongest group of NCOs here. Yates, your company is strong. As for the rest of us, who knows?"

"The general put Reno in charge of some training," Cooke told. "Marksmanship and more horsemanship has been implemented."

"Let Jimmi here tell you what Reynolds told him," said Moylan. "That's what has my hair standing up."

Lieutenant James Calhoun, was a brother-in-law to the general and Tom Custer, liked by all for his easy demeanor. He was no stranger to fighting. During the war, he'd fought as an enlisted man and earned an officer's commission. At times, he could be shy, especially around the older officers of the regiment. He looked at the floor, uneasy with the attention now focused on him.

"Go on, Jimmi," urged Moylan.

Calhoun looked up at the assembled group. "We were doing some hunting the other day, me and Reynolds. He'd just come in after spending some time alone out on the plains. I guess he ran into several groups of Indians. He said he had to hide out a few times on account of so many Indians between here and the Powder." Calhoun hesitated; a nervous look rippled across his face. "Well, anyway, he said something to the effect that he had never in all his years out here encountered so many Indians that he feared for his life."

Keogh's mind raced. The harsh reality of the frontier Army was now upon them with precious little time before the Seventh went out on campaign. New recruits, with very little training were the norm in any Army outfit on the Plains. Keogh, as well as the other officers, all knew that, in a fight, precautions would have to be taken.

He scanned the faces in the room, wondering if the others were as worried as he. If an experienced plainsman like Charles Reynolds was concerned, they all should be. The past had taught him how unpredictable and violent Indian encounters could be, but he masked his doubts under false bravado, hoping none could see through the act. Most of the Seventh's officers were veterans of the war, but few had substantial Indian fights under their belts, a fact which concerned Keogh greatly. For many in the regiment, this would be their first taste of Indian warfare.

To hell with these feelings, Keogh. This is the Fighting Seventh! No group of Indians will be our demise. Don't you go forgetting, you rode in over forty battles in the war. You were at Gettysburg. You were a prisoner of war.

~

At times like these, his mind uneasy, Keogh would go to Comanche. He and the horse had been together for eight years now. Just seeing the animal's reaction when he caught site of Keogh, made him feel calm. Together, they'd fought Indians in Kansas and throughout the Indian Territory. There had been some close calls.

105

The horse had been wounded a few times, including the time when he saved Keogh's life.

"There you are," said Keogh as he patted Comanche's face.

The horse raised his head up and down, immediately smelling the treats Keogh had brought for him. The horse pushed his hand away and sniffed him.

"Ok, ok. Here are your apples."

Saddled and eager to stretch his legs, Comanche carried Keogh over the rolling hills surrounding the fort. The horse had natural instincts and would climb any hill without being prompted. Keogh never had to jerk the reins, he simply used his legs to indicate a change in directions. Comanche seemed to be able to sense when a situation warranted action. He was rugged, tough and fearless---and he loved Myles Keogh.

On a hill overlooking the Missouri River, Keogh halted Comanche. A gentle wind blew across the plains. "One last time out, old friend," he told the horse. "Then we go to Nelly, forever."

Two
11 May 1876

"Attention!" shouted Sergeant Major William Sharrow, United States Seventh Cavalry.

Keogh and his fellow officers stood at attention. General George Custer swept into the room, followed closely by Tom and Cooke.

George Custer was now thirty-six, still lean and full of self-confidence. He had remained in the public eye as the Seventh Cavalry cleared the Southern Plains of hostile Indian tribes. For his efforts Custer was given the distinction as the best Indian fighter the Army had and the Seventh Cavalry the best Indian fighting regiment on the frontier.

On the trail chasing Indians, he was relentless and determined. He pushed the Seventh through all kinds of weather and terrain, which at times left both men and animals health in jeopardy.

No matter the tribes, or their numbers, Custer believed the Seventh could defeat them all. The only problem the Army saw in fighting Indians was finding them and bringing them to battle.

"At ease, gentlemen," said General Custer. "Lieutenant Cooke, proceed."

The lieutenant stepped to the front. "January 31, 1876, by order of the War Department. All non-treaty Indians are hereby ordered to report to the nearest agency on the double, or be considered a hostile enemy to the United States of America."

"Thank you, Cooke. Gentlemen, as you know, I have been gone for some time with the hearings in Washington, D.C.," General Custer said. "Back in February, I was in Saint Paul with General Terry. We were ordered to begin devising a plan that will take the Seventh into the field to bring the Sioux and the other hostiles to their knees, once and for all."

The men of the Seventh Cavalry waited in silence. All present had known this day was coming. Keogh looked to his right at Benteen. Still the elder statesman among the Seventh Cavalry's officers, the captain was emotionless and stoic as ever.

"The Sioux are believed to be west of the Little Missouri River. They may even be somewhere in the vicinity of the Powder River, over in Montana territory with some Cheyenne bands," continued General Custer. "We will move west in an effort to link up with the other two units in the field. General Crook will be making his way up from Wyoming territory and General Gibbon will be coming east from Fort Ellis. Between the three units we shall be able to snare the hostiles somewhere below the Yellowstone."

The general's plan was now out in the open for all to grasp.

"We will have seasoned scouts to lead us," said the general. "Gentlemen, I would like to introduce four men whom many of you already know."

Sergeant Major Sharrow opened the door. Three civilians and one Indian walked in. The civilians were plainsman and familiar to most in the regiment. The Indian was an Arikara. He was the general's favorite scout.

"Gentlemen, for those of you who don't know these men, let me do the honors," General Custer said. "This is Mr. Frederic Gerard and Mr. Isaiah Dorman. Both know the Sioux, their language and the territory west of the Missouri. Both are friends to the Arikara, enemy of the Sioux. Next is my friend, Bloody Knife. He is an Arikara scout." The General nodded his head to Bloody Knife, who respectfully returned the gesture. "Lastly, this is Mr. Charles Reynolds. He's been in the territory between the Little Missouri River and the Powder River this past spring and has some interesting news for us."

General Custer motioned Charles Reynolds forward. The plainsman stepped up to address the officers. He seemed a quiet man, shy in a way, but most considered him the best hunter in the

Dakota Territory. College educated, he'd left school to fight in the war. He traveled alone most of the time, giving him the nickname, Lonesome Charley.

"Hello. I recognize a great many of you," Reynolds said. "I can tell you with certainty that the Sioux have no intention of going to the reservations and they are encouraging other tribes to join them in defiance. Over in the Montana Territory, I am being told by other Indians the Cheyenne have had enough as well. All want to be left alone, to the old ways. They will fight if it comes to it. In all my years on the plains, I have never heard or seen anything of the like."

"Good, and thank you all," said General Custer. "If the Sioux and Cheyenne are wanting a fight, then all we have to do is find them. We'll travel with a wagon train until the trail is struck. Each company should be ready to move out immediately when the order is given. I am depending on you all as troop commanders to have your companies ready at a moment's notice."

Keogh closed his eyes. All he could see was Nelly. The general's announcement of a large campaign left him with a mix of emotions. He could now give Nelly an idea of when he'd return. He'd promised this was his last time out chasing Indians. Relieved and ready for action, the chance to prove himself was now upon him. Nothing else mattered. He was going with his regiment on one last adventure. He had to prove he was still a soldier.

This is it, Keogh. Something big will come of this.

The announcement meant the United States Seventh Cavalry would be in the field by the summer of 1876. For the first time in the regiment's history, all twelve companies would ride together. A thought occurred to Keogh as he sat waiting for the meeting to adjourn. The United States of America, his adopted country, the country he had sworn to fight and die for, if needed, would be celebrating its one hundred year anniversary that summer.

There you go, Keogh. Lady Luck has delivered you a grand opportunity.

Three
17 May 1876

Keogh awoke from the dream, startled and confused. He grabbed his pocket watch. To his relief, the hands indicated three o'clock in the morning. The lone candle's light flickered and cast shadows from where it sat on the table, each flutter further stoking his nerves.

He laid back down and tried to remember his dream, tried to make sense of it. All he could recall was being accompanied by soldiers with whom he'd served in both wars, Keily and O'Keefe included. Many of those faces he'd not thought of in years. Then it came to him. All were dead now!

Thoughts of what the dream meant swirled in a mix of confusion and apprehension.

Snap out of it. It's only a dream. The dead are dead, leave them buried. They have nothing to do with this campaign…nothing! Everything is going to be fine. Get up and get moving.

One task remained before he started his day. It was time to write Nelly. He took out pencil and paper in hopes that the right words would come.

My Dearest Nelly,

We leave this morning for our big Indian campaign. I will try to write to you from the field if we are out for an extended period of time. We hope to find the hostiles somewhere in the territory of the Powder River. If we don't, we will keep pushing west until we find them. A newspaper man travels with us, whom I am sure will do his best to get our story out to all the papers.

It's a funny thing when a man finds a woman like you, yet must constantly be away from her company. I now know, as I sit here in the early morning darkness, that I no longer want this lonely Army life that I've come to know for so long. I want to thank you for being patient and waiting on me. I promise, when I return and find myself in your arms, I'll be the one waiting on you from now on.

I feel good and ready for this journey. All twelve companies of the Seventh Cavalry will be together in the field. We have many experienced officers and good men among us. I must admit, I do worry about our enlisted men. Their training and fighting abilities could be tested if we find any Indians. I hope we don't find ourselves in a tight situation on the trail, but I'll do my best to keep my men safe. Hopefully, we'll surprise the hostiles, and maybe a show of force will convince them to come in.

I must finish for now, my time is running out. My company is ready and eager to get moving. I want you to know that your family has been like my own over these past years. I don't know what would have become of me, had I not met you. It is my love for you that prompts me to ask. If I should be killed, it is my wish to be packed up and sent to you to be buried at your family's home. I hope you have always known that you alone are what I hold dear in this world.

Please don't worry too much, Nelly. I am confident Comanche will look out for me. I have not forgotten what you told me that day on the porch. Please remember that, should things turn out bad, I did everything I could to get back to you. I am a soldier, and sometimes soldiers don't make it home. I have loved and will always love you. I am counting the days until I no longer have to remember what you look like, but instead, can merely cast my eyes upon you.

Love forever,

Myles

~

Five-thirty in the morning. Time to go.

Keogh stepped out of his quarters and was met by I Company First Sergeant, Frank Varden. The sergeant was stout, with a barrel chest and big arms. He was the type of non-commissioned officer a company commander needed in a frontier unit, tough, reliable

112

and more than capable to lead men.

"Good morning, first sergeant."

"Morning, captain."

"How are the men this morning? All present and accounted for?"

"Yes, captain, all are ready for inspection. Damn cold, foggy morning, sir."

"Good, let's get to it. Six o'clock is fast approaching." Keogh felt for the Angus Dei necklace about his neck, panicking a moment before his fingers brushed the chain. The religious medal had been a gift from his mother before he left Ireland.

Seek God's protection in times of trouble.

They moved for the ground on which I Company stood assembled. All throughout Fort Lincoln, commands were given and roll calls were underway as the other eleven companies gathered for their inspections. Keogh and Varden stopped in front of the company.

"Attention!" shouted I Company Sergeant James Bustard. With the command, forty-four troopers snapped to attention.

Varden joined the company's other sergeants, Bustard and Milton Delacy. The three stood next to First Lieutenant James Porter. This would be the lieutenant's first time leading men on an Indian campaign.

I Company's dog, Joe, wondered in and out of the ranks. The dog would routinely accompany the troop whenever they went into the field or anywhere else. It appeared he wasn't going to miss out on this journey.

Dressed to take the field, the men of I Company looked ready for a campaign. Their pants were a light blue, with leather sewn throughout the seat and inner thighs to prevent rubbing. Most troopers wore the dark blue, wide-brimmed Army issue hat. Some preferred a gray or white hat, though, and had purchased them on their own.

Each trooper carried a Colt .45 revolver, an ammunition belt, and a knife; a black leather strap was slung cross the chest with a clip attached to the band to support each soldier's rifle.

As Keogh reviewed his troops, his heart swelled with pride.

Now, this is what a cavalry troop should look like.

When the troopers began to holler and then cheer, Keogh was caught off guard. Many grabbed their hats and waived them. He turned to see what had caused the commotion.

It was Comanche.

The horse was led by I Company's Blacksmith, Henry Bailey. Comanche pranced, pulled on the lead rope held by the blacksmith and danced his way to Keogh's side. The men hurrahed, and Comanche tossed his head up and down.

"We had a hell of a time with him this morning," said Bailey. "I think he thought we were leaving without him. After some time, we just let him out of his stall. He followed us and the rest of the men around all morning. When it came time to leave, we still had not put his bridle and bit on, so we let Private Symms try," Bailey laughed as he told more. "Ole Comanche, he wasn't about to let some private put his hands on him."

The troopers chuckled at the blacksmith's remarks. Keogh figured Comanche's behavior had been a welcomed distraction for his men.

"It took both Symms and Private Lloyd to get him ready," Bailey added.

Keogh smiled then rubbed Comanche's ears and patted his neck. "Okay, boy. We're not leaving you behind." Comanche looked him in the eyes and, for a brief moment, Keogh felt something strange. The horse's eyes seemed bigger than usual and he watched every move Keogh made. The strange feelings came again, only this time it was a sense of sadness. "Easy, old friend. Our last time out, I promise. Then I take you to Nelly."

Satisfied with his inspection, Keogh handed the reins back to

Bailey. He pulled himself onto Paddy, wanting Comanche fresh for when the trail was struck. "I Company, United States Seventh Cavalry, mount up!" he shouted.

~

The Seventh Cavalry made twelve miles the first day out, moving west along the Heart River. The next morning, Keogh and his fellow officers witnessed the general in a manner few had ever seen him.

General Custer's wife, Libby, had accompanied the regiment to this point. Before continuing on, the couple said a heart-felt goodbye. All the officers in the Seventh knew he loved his wife but had never seen him show such affection. As the entire regiment watched Libby Custer's escort start back to Fort Lincoln, Benteen rode to where Keogh sat. "The man almost appears human, wouldn't you say, Keogh?"

"Not sure, Benteen. I got an uneasy feeling about just what he intends to do, should we find us a trail."

"You should have misgivings. They all should. Like I told you back in the Indian Territory. Make no mistake of the man's intentions, Keogh. The hour will soon be at hand, and God help us if he has the choice of playing it safe or taking us all to hell."

Four
1 June 1876
Dakota Territory

From the outset, General Custer and one company of cavalry rode out front of the Dakota Column to scout the way. Following them were two companies riding in support and assigned to build bridges if needed. Thirty-seven Arikara Indian scouts, led by Lieutenant Charles Varnum, rode in a sweeping ark before the regiment. The Arikara were once a thriving tribe, mighty warriors, and formidable as any Indians on the Plains. Constantly harassed by the Sioux, the Arikaras had jumped at the chance to scout for the Army and fight against their old enemy.

At the head of the wagon train rode the Dakota Columns' overall commander, General Alfred Terry. He and his staff were followed by three companies of infantry, consisting of one-hundred and forty men, eighty new recruits without horses and the Gatlin Gun detachment. One hundred and fifty wagons in all, pulled by mules and horses, carried the supplies and extra ammunition for the entire regiment.

Three companies of cavalry were assigned duty to escort and help the wagons when necessary. They would gather wood for the evening camp, as well as guard the back of the Dakota Column.

At one side of the wagon train, the pack animals and extra mounts were herded. On the other, the cattle trudged along. Each flank, five hundred yards out, had three companies protecting the herds and wagons. Each company had outriders posted at all times.

It was slow going as the regiment crawled toward the Little Missouri River. The weather, always a force to be reckoned with, impeded their progress further when the rain turned to snow over the next four days. When the Seventh reached the badlands of the Little Missouri River, the flat, grassy plains disappeared into a rough and unforgiving landscape.

There had been very few signs of Indian trails over the one hundred and fifty miles the Seventh had traveled so far. Messengers from Gibbon's command, to the west in Montana Territory, had reported that large numbers of Sioux were somewhere south of the Yellowstone River.

The Seventh spent the days traveling the rough badlands and the nights resting. The troops settled into the evening routine of inspecting, then picketing their horses. Dinner was followed by card games and socialization around each company's fires.

Keogh liked to spend his evenings around the fire listening and talking to Benteen, Captain McDougall, Moylan, Captain French, Porter, Mathey and DeRudio. Many in the group had seen considerable action. Their stories still fascinated one another.

Lieutenant DeRudio's tales never ceased to amaze those who listened. "I said, DeRudio, if they sentence you to Devil's Island, you're done for."

"You mean to tell us you were sentenced and then escaped from Devil's Island?" asked Moylan.

"That is correct, sir."

"DeRudio, or should I say, Count No Account?" said Benteen. "You are something, you know that?"

"Enough of your stories, DeRudio," McDougall said. "Keogh, tell us about Gettysburg, or marching through Georgia with Sherman."

Keogh waited to respond. He closed his eyes. His story was unique. Different from the others, he knew. The rest of the Seventh's officers considered him somewhat a ladies' man, with Nelly back east from a wealthy and prestigious family waiting on him. A veteran of not only one, but two wars, Keogh's devil may care attitude personified his image as a hard charging cavalry officer. He had ridden in so many engagements in the war and on the Plains, and had come through them all without ever being wounded. What truly set him apart from the rest and only added to the legend, was that he rode in the Seventh for the adventure.

Keogh's mind raced back to the places and names that so long ago had made up his world.

The war. Now, that was being a soldier. I lived a dream.

He stayed in his thoughts, thinking of all those he had forgotten. The battles, the death and destruction, all of it came racing back.

They want you to tell them everything will be fine. Put their minds at ease. Look at them; they're counting on you.

"Keogh, you awake over there?" asked McDougall.

"Yes, yes. I am awake."

"What about it, then?" French pleaded.

Tell them a good one.

"Did I ever tell you boys about my journey to Gettysburg?" he began. "Well, the whole time me and General Buford are marching north, I'm on my own secret mission."

He had them, and for a short time, the worrisome thoughts left him.

Five
9 June 1876
Powder River
Montana Territory

"Officers' call, captain. General Custer's tent," said Sharrow. "Sixteen hundred hours."

The appearance of the sergeant major caught the attention of the group of officers sitting with Keogh. All listened.

"What's the latest, sergeant major?" asked Keogh.

Sharrow glanced at the officers, then looked directly at Keogh, "Captain."

"Easy Sharrow," Keogh said. "You are among friends here."

"It started before we came into the Powder River Valley," Sharrow told. "General Terry made a big to--- do about Reynolds not knowing the territory well enough. Told General Custer that, if we don't make better time, Indians are going to slip away on us."

"I see," said Keogh. "What did Reynolds say?"

"Nothing. Took it like he was a soldier," Sharrow said.

"Did either that pencil pusher Terry or our boy general think Reynolds might just know what he's doing?" Benteen asked. The captain had been quiet, up till now, agitation hardening his tone. "Just like Custer not to stand up for someone keeping him from hurrying into a mess."

"So, where did Terry go?" asked Captain French.

"General Terry took two companies, Captain Moylan's and Yate's company, over to Gibbon's base camp at the mouth of the Powder," said Sharrow. "Said that, since Reynolds can't find his way, he'd bring some help. General Custer told Reynolds not to worry. Said he will get us cut free from General Terry soon as we strike a big trail."

121

"Is General Terry back yet?" McDougall asked.

"Yes, captain," answered Sharrow.

~

General Terry exited the tent to find the Seventh Cavalry's officers waiting on him.

"Attention," announced Sharrow.

"At ease, gentleman," ordered Terry.

Keogh and his fellow officers relaxed. They watched General Terry move to a small table where General Custer waited with a map.

"I have news and a plan for the Seventh," Terry told. "I have just returned from our temporary base camp at the mouth of the Powder. It was there I made contact with Gibbon's column. Other than some early contact with the Sioux, there has been no sign of the hostiles for two weeks now. It is believed they are somewhere in the vicinity of the Tongue River or Rosebud. We have not gotten any word from General Crook and his Wyoming column moving from the south. A reconnaissance is needed." He looked at General Custer.

"Major Reno, you will lead the reconnaissance," Custer said. "Your orders are precise and exact."

Reno glared at Custer. His dislike for the man was easy for Keogh and the others to see. It made him uneasy to think the major couldn't hold his contempt for the general while the regiment was on campaign, in the heart of enemy territory.

I hope to God Benteen and the general can get through this without some type of altercation.

In return, Custer smirked as he gave the major his orders. "Major, you and your command are to ascend the Powder and cross to the headwaters of Mizpah Creek. From there, descend that creek to its junction with the Powder River and then cross Pumpkin

122

Creek and the Tongue River. Descend the Tongue to its junction with the Yellowstone. Once there, you will rejoin us at a new supply depot." His voiced took on a sharp edge. "You are to avoid discovery by any hostiles. Stay away from the Rosebud. You will receive a written copy of the orders, plus a map of the territory." He paused and looked at General Terry. "With your permission, sir?"

"Go on, Custer."

"The Seventh has a new guide." General Custer looked in the direction of Reynolds, who stood nearby with Dorman, Gerard, Bloody Knife, and a stranger. "Gentlemen, this is Mister Boyer. Mitch Boyer, to be exact. He has been trained by the legendary Jim Bridger, and General Terry has enlisted his aid. He knows the territory and the Sioux well."

"Thank you, Custer," said General Terry. "Gentleman, let me be clear. We are in hostile territory. That is all. Dismissed."

At the conclusion of the meeting, the officers who had been picked for the reconnaissance mission milled about. Major Reno had instructions and assignments. Other officers stayed and listened.

"Well, Reno, now you got yourself a command. Try not to get these boys killed out there, will you?" said Benteen.

"I will do what my orders tell me to do, Benteen," Reno said as he glared at the captain. The major gathered his composure and issued orders. "Yates, you will have Companies E, L and your F. Keogh, you get B, C and your I Company. We will have rations for twelve days and a train of seventy mules, along with one Gatlin Gun."

The mission was anything but sure. The thought of separating the regiment in the heart of hostile territory made Keogh's stomach churn. From his time with the major, he knew Reno was careful when it came to matters concerning troops and their overall safety. He also knew that Reno played it cautious when chasing Indians. They had better be careful, if Reynolds was right. At least

Yates, McDougall and Calhoun would be going. They were men Keogh felt he could depend on if a fight occurred. It still didn't matter, though, despite the strong group of officers picked, Keogh's mind was uneasy.

Six

Major Reno had the six companies in his command on the move by three-thirty in the afternoon the following day. Two long days of riding over country full of gullies and steep hills covered with pine trees brought them to the Tongue River. The new scout, Boyer, had sent two of the Arikara scouts back to Reno.

At Boyer's request, Keogh, along with Captains Yates, Mc-Dougall and the major, trotted away from the command with a small detachment of troopers to see something.

They stopped in a meadow not far from the river. Boyer and some of the Arikara examined the ground. Keogh and the others dismounted, then walked ahead. Boyer showed them the site of a recent Indian camp.

Reno moved through the discarded camp material and debris. "How many lodges you guess, Boyer?" he asked.

The scout looked at an Arikara and communicated through sign language. Nodding his head, Boyer turned his attention to Reno. "Four hundred, maybe more."

The answer caught Keogh's attention. He knew from his time on the Plains that estimate meant there was at least six hundred warriors within this camp, maybe more. A number almost equal to that of the entire Seventh's fighting force!

Yates and McDougall continued their inspection of the campsite. "How far are we behind them, would you say?" Yates asked.

"This camp will have moved two, maybe even three times already," said Boyer. "The camp has too many people and horses to stay in the same spot too long. They're heading west."

"How many warriors?" asked Reno.

"Enough to handle us right here and now!"

Boyer's words were heard by all.

Keogh glanced at Yates, then McDougall. Both had started to

move back to their horses. None wanted to be out in the open, should any warriors still be lurking behind.

The scouts and Boyer followed Reno's group back to their horses. The major stopped before mounting. "Boyer, take some of the scouts, follow their trail."

~

By the seventh day out, Boyer and the scouts had found a large, fresh trail. It led toward the Rosebud River. The major had been instructed to keep away from the Rosebud so not to alert any Indians of the Seventh's presence but deemed the trail too important to let go without reconnoitering. Reno reasoned Terry and General Custer would want to know the hostiles were in the Rosebud Valley. He sent the scouts to investigate.

Boyer and the scouts followed the trail as it turned to the south, up the valley. It led to an abandoned campsite.

Once back with the soldiers and Reno, Boyer had plenty to tell. "I'm telling you all now, these here Indians are not leaving, but are converging into one damn big village."

"So, you believe more Indians have not only joined, but more are following?" Keogh asked.

The scout nodded somberly as an Arikara approached and spoke to him. "Forked Horn, here, says the hostile village is not more than a day's ride from here."

"We're that close?" asked an excited Reno.

"Hold on, major!" Boyer cautioned. "The Arikara say that, if the Sioux see us, the sun will not move very far before we are all killed."

Every officer was silent. They understood the major was looking to prove himself in the eyes of General Terry, to show General Custer he was a worthy choice to lead such a reconnaissance. He wanted to find the hostiles, or at least learn of their approximate location.

Keogh wished to caution the major but knew better than to offer advice before being asked.

I wish the entire regiment was together.

Reno cleared his throat. "Captain Yates, how would you sum up the commands condition as of now?"

"In the shape we're in, not good enough to be taking on a village of that size," Yates said. "Our horses are just about played out and the Gatlin Gun is giving us fits."

"What say you, Keogh?" asked Reno.

All eyes shifted towards Keogh. He felt the stares and knew the reason. He was the senior captain, the only officer there who could reason with Reno.

Keogh watched Boyer. The scout looked at the ground, then kicked at the grass.

He's nervous. Something's not right.

"We should not attack them now, major," he said. "If the whole regiment was together, then I would say yes, but not now. We don't have enough men or extra ammunition."

Reno said nothing at first, lost in his thoughts. "Let us return to the assigned rendezvous area and report. We have accomplished our mission without giving away our position. There is no need to risk it."

Seven
21 June 1876
Yellowstone River

The Seventh Cavalry had reunited at its new supply camp, just below the Yellowstone River. A steamer, the *Far West,* was moored on the river and served as a command base for General Terry. General Custer and the Montana Column commander, Colonel John Gibbon, had met Terry to discuss Reno's report. With the Indians general vicinity now known, operations for a coordinated attack were planned.

Exhausted and worn down from the reconnaissance mission, Keogh tried to get some rest and nourishment. For most of the trip, the Seventh had been able to hunt game to supplement their rations. Now, deep in hostile territory, they'd been existing on hardtack crackers, bacon, water and coffee, with beans mixed in when time allowed.

Keogh got himself moving. He had to check on his men before the briefing with the general. He wouldn't let the negative thoughts and nervous energy swirling in his head regarding the number of warriors the Seventh could encounter, keep eating at him. His unwavering confidence in his and the regiment's fighting abilities had been reaffirmed. They'd survived the mission deep in the heart of enemy territory and it had proved a success. He had to keep reminding himself, this would be his last campaign.

There will be something in return for all my years out here.

~

General Custer addressed the officers. "Gentlemen, I have new orders for the Fighting Seventh," he announced. "We are to ride up the Rosebud, to its headwaters, and continue south past the Indian

129

trail. If the trail is found to diverge westward, we'll move over to the Little Bighorn and down that river. We will seek the Indians out and drive them into the Montana column."

Several officers voiced questions at the same time. General Custer raised his hand and all talking ceased. "We leave tomorrow with Crow and a scout by the name of Herendeen."

George Herendeen was a seasoned plainsman. He knew the territory west of the Rosebud, as well as the Little Bighorn Valley.

The Crow knew the territory where the hostile Indians were thought to be roaming. The Powder and Tongue Rivers were their homeland, a territory that had long ago become a battleground between them and the Cheyenne. The Crow had fought the invasion with ferocity but bands of Sioux were now encroaching on their lands in search of new hunting grounds. The Crow were fierce warriors and considered by many to be the finest horsemen of all the Plains tribes.

General Custer eyed the officers. "We will strip down to the essentials, with each troop commander responsible for his own company. We will take the mules from the wagons and use them for our pack train. Each trooper will carry fifteen days of rations. The regimental band will be left behind with one-hundred and fifty men. You have your orders. That is all."

After the meeting Keogh completed more of his designated rounds. He moved for I Company's campsite, worried about the company's horses and, of course, Comanche and Paddy. The regiment had been in the field for over a month now, with little rest and on half rations at times for the animals.

Keogh and the company's sergeants inspected the horses for any signs of saddle sores or problems with their ankles and hooves. Considering all the horses had been through, they were in relatively good condition. Paddy and Comanche were better off than most, as Keogh alternated riding between Paddy and other extra mounts the regiment had brought along. He continued to keep Comanche with the company, yet he didn't ride him. A fresh horse could be all the difference between life or death in the fight that was sure to come.

With some free time now, Keogh made his way to the regimental headquarters unit. He wanted to talk to Cooke.

Throughout the campaign, something had seemed wrong with the lieutenant. Keogh had even noticed something odd with his friend before the journey had begun. He couldn't recall what exactly it was that caught his attention, but Cooke acted more reserved and distant than usual.

Just a ways from Cooke's tent, Keogh heard the lieutenant discussing what he assumed were his responsibilities as adjutant.

"I need you two to act as my witnesses," said Cooke.

"Oh, Cookie, go on with that, will you?" Lieutenant Jack Sturgis replied.

"What gives?" Lieutenant Francis Gibson asked. "This isn't like you?"

"There's nothing wrong with me," said Cooke. "Just got a bad feeling we might get into a fight out here, that's all. Besides, I've been putting it off for far too long."

With his presence undetected, Keogh continued listening outside the tent. He was shocked at what he had just heard Cooke say. The lieutenant was one of toughest soldiers he'd ever known. He had fought in the war and survived numerous fights with Indians over the years.

What has him so scared that he wants his will drafted now?

Keogh didn't bother Cooke. Instead, he headed for the officers he'd spent most of his time with along the campaign. When he found their campsite, he stopped some distance away and listened to the chatter. As usual, DeRudio was doing most of the talking. The regulars were all there, along with some new faces. All seemed glad to be sharing a fire.

"I said to my fellow conspirators, if we should pull off this endeavor, mankind shall be that much better off," DeRudio said.

"Just how in the hell, did you stumble your way into a plot to kill Napoleon?" asked French.

Keogh neared the fire.

"Well, look who it is, boys. It's none other than my favorite Irishman," said Benteen.

"Do sit down and join us, Keogh," French said. "DeRudio here was just about to tell us how he managed to get himself in on a plot to kill Napoleon."

"I was listening. I didn't want to miss out on this one," Keogh said.

"You just missed General Custer, himself," said Benteen.

"I'm sure he stopped by to hear a good story or two," Keogh replied.

Once the laughter died down, no one spoke. Some smoked; others drank coffee. All gazed at the fire, lost in their thoughts. Keogh scanned their faces. His companions were worried, their anxiety crackling like electricity in the air.

Tell them it will be okay. They trust you.

"Well, by what the scouts say, it looks like it won't be long before we're all bragging about having fought some Indians. That is, if we catch the hostiles before they scatter," he said.

No words or questions were returned.

"Keogh, before you got here, Custer gave me grief for shooting an Indian boy at the Washita," Benteen said.

All eyes were on Benteen now.

"I'm sure you set him straight," Keogh answered.

"You're damn right I did. I told that son-of-a-bitch that, if we get in a tight spot out there, I hope he supports us better than he supported Elliot!"

Silence hung in the air, disrupted only by the popping embers of the fire. Bits and pieces of ash floated into the night sky.

"Let's go, boys," said McDougall. "We have men and animals

to check on once more."

"Yes, we all need to be shoving off," Moylan said.

One by one, they left, back to their respective companies, until only Keogh and Benteen remained by the fire.

"Has the general gotten under your skin that much, or is something else bothering you tonight?"

"You know what's bothering me, Keogh. That damned fool is taking us right to hell; we both see it. I hope to God, he don't split the regiment up out there if he finds any damn Indians. Mark my words, my friend. When the hour comes, and it will come, we all better hope and pray to God Almighty that we're not too far from one another!"

A sick, bitter sensation crept into Keogh's stomach. From the beginning of the campaign, he'd felt uneasy. Hearing Benteen mentioning the Washita only added to his worries…

All your dreams!

Benteen had only said what the others thought. The Arikara scouts, Boyer, Cooke, Reynolds---all had voiced their apprehension. His thoughts turned to Nelly and to their last conversation.

"Don't you try to save all of them from going to hell."

"Get some sleep, Keogh. Something tells me we're in for some very long and hard days."

Eight
22 June 1876

"If you ever find yourself in a bad way out there--- and I mean so bad that, no matter how hard you try, it's not going to work---you let Comanche carry you away and don't look back. Don't you look back! Just the two of you run back here to me. Don't you try to save all of them!"

Keogh opened his eyes and looked up at the night sky. The stars shone like diamonds and it was as if Nelly had spoken to him through them. He laid on a blanket with his saddle at his back.

God, I'm so tired and sore.

The dream left him unsettled, a nervous feeling scratching at his mind and stomach.

Snap out of it. You are the captain of this company. Get moving and show nothing to anyone.

After inspecting I Company's horses, Keogh headed to breakfast. Already eating and waiting on him were the company's sergeants and Porter.

"Good morning, captain," said Varden.

"How are the men this morning?" Keogh asked. "Do we still number forty-four?"

"Yes, captain," Varden replied. "None have taken the grand bounce yet."

"Hopefully, we'll find the Indians before any of our horses give out," Bustard said.

"I couldn't agree with you more, sergeant," said Keogh. "Just make sure the men are doing everything they can for their horses. I don't see us resting for the next week."

"General Custer is determined to find that village and have us a fight. Even if none of us has a horse to ride into it, isn't he, captain?" Delacy asked.

"It would appear that way, sergeant," Keogh replied. "You four make sure you don't let the men hear or see your concern. We don't want to give them any excuse to fall out when the action gets a little hot."

~

By noon, the Seventh Cavalry departed the supply camp on the Yellowstone River. General Terry made sure to send them off in grand fashion. The Seventh's regimental band played the tune *Garry Owen* when each company passed by Terry for review. He'd decided to ride with Gibbon's command now. They would act as a blocking force, coming up the Little Bighorn River.

General Custer and the Seventh Cavalry had been cut loose to chase Indians.

At the head of the twelve companies, General Custer rode with the regimental headquarters unit. There was Tom Custer, riding as an aide-de-camp, and Cooke, the Seventh's Adjutant. Following along were Sergeant Major Sharrow, Chief Trumpeter Henry Voss and Chief Surgeon, First Lieutenant George Lord. Color Sergeant John Vickory carried the Seventh Cavalry's Regimental Stars and Stripes flag. Color Sergeant Robert Hughes carried General Custer's personal headquarters battle flag, a swallow tail guidon of red over blue with crossed sabers. Directly behind the two flag bearing sergeants rode a couple of trumpeters, chosen on a daily basis to serve as the general's orderlies. Boston Custer, the general and Tom's younger brother, and their nephew Autie Reed completed the group. The two had come along in search of some adventure.

Ranging far ahead of the regiment were the six Crow scouts, Boyer, and Lieutenant Varnum. The lieutenant was one of the regiment's most capable young officers. The Arikara scouts rode on the regiment's flanks to ensure no side trails were missed. Lieutenant Luther Hare, another young and promising officer, rode with the Arikara, as did four Sioux scouts.

The plainsmen, Herendeen, Reynolds, Dorman and Gerard rode near the general and the headquarters unit at all times. Bloody Knife and two other young scouts, Billy Jackson and Billy Cross, rode close as well. Mark Kellogg, a newspaper reporter who had accompanied the campaign from the beginning, now found himself riding his mule to report on whatever lay ahead for the Fighting Seventh Cavalry.

The regiment followed the Rosebud, crossing it and then having to re-cross it on several occasions because of the surrounding terrain. The pack train, now consisting of the mules pulled from the wagons, fell far behind from the start. It was exhausting work, keeping the mules moving and the packs on them. What had started out as such an exciting day, full of suspense and excitement to be back on the trail, had now turned into a slow reminder of just how hard it is to travel with pack animals.

Plodding along on Paddy, Keogh's mind raced, obsessing over his disappointing career following the war.

Jesus Christ, Keogh, what have you been doing out here all these years?

A verse from Charles O'Malley, The Irish Dragoon, came to him.

A brooding melancholy gained daily more and more upon me. A wish to return to Ireland---a vague and indistinct feeling that my career was not destined for ought of great and good, crept upon me, and I longed to sink into oblivion, forgotten and forgot.

No, something big is coming. This is why you stayed in the Army, for just such a campaign. An epic journey for an epic ending. You're in it now. Get your mind right. Seize the day.

Nine
Rosebud Valley

It was four in the afternoon when the Seventh stopped, having covered twelve miles. That night after supper, Keogh found himself by the fire listening to DeRudio tell more stories. Benteen, French, McDougall, Mathey and some other junior officers were close by. The mood was festive, in a quiet way. Everyone knew the regiment was close to striking a fresh trail. They'd followed several smaller ones, all seemingly heading in the same direction and merging into one big one.

"DeRudio, to hear you tell it, you'd think you were royalty. Yet, here you are with us," said Benteen. "I think you're full of it."

"I'm just telling the story of my life, captain. Each man is free to choose whether he believes it or not," DeRudio replied.

Benteen held a cup of coffee, "Oh, I see." After a long drink, he paused. "Well, you're still Count No Account to me."

Keogh hardly listened to the banter or stories. He was tired, and he knew he should get some sleep. Four o'clock in the morning would be upon them soon. His thoughts returned to Nelly. He couldn't wait to be out of the Army and by her side. He closed his eyes and tried to recall her face.

"Officers' call. Officers' call at the general's tent!" announced Sharrow.

When the Sergeant Major called for you, it was something serious. Already, several officers had made their way to the group where Keogh sat.

"What in the hell is it now?" asked an angry Moylan.

"What does it matter?" said French. "You got to go and hear what the man says."

The group of officers and Keogh stumbled through the dark camp. Small fires from each company's supper, now reduced to embers, provided the only light. There, waiting for them outside the general's tent, was Tom and Cooke.

"What gives, Cooke?" Moylan asked.

"The general has some important information and orders for us," he replied.

General Custer stepped out of his tent and moved to a small table. The lone lantern's light lit his unshaven face against the black night. Custer, who usually kept his blond hair long and curly, had cut his locks short before starting out on the campaign. It was only now starting to grow back and show its color.

"Gentlemen, I have called you here by way of the sergeant major, as we will be using no more bugle calls except if the situation warrants. Make no mistake, we are in enemy territory. Our orders are to follow the hostile's trail, wherever it takes us. I am depending on you senior and junior officers to follow each order down to the letter. Our mission will depend on it. The regiment must stay hidden until the time is right to attack. Lieutenant Cooke, if you please?"

Cooke moved into the lantern's light. "Lieutenant Wallace is the acting engineering officer. Wallace, proceed."

Second Lieutenant George Wallace stepped forward. Wallace was tall and lanky, his demeanor serious. "Gentlemen, please set your watches to Chicago time, on my count. Set your watches to twenty-two hundred hours, now."

"Anything else, sir?" Cooke asked.

"Yes. I'm not happy with the performance of the pack train and mules today. Lieutenant Mathey, from now on, you will be in charge of the mules and the packers," ordered General Custer. "Starting tomorrow morning, the last company to report at the ready will be rewarded with escort duty for the pack train."

The general studied all in attendance. He put his right hand on his holstered revolver and then settled his left hand on the knife encased in its scabbard on his belt. "If any of you have any suggestions, bring them to my attention. We could end up fighting more warriors than ever imagined. I am depending on you all and so is your regiment. Dismissed."

The meeting left more than one officer confused. To Keogh, the general's tone and disposition were unlike any he had experienced with him before. For a man who was always so self-assured when it came to fighting, it was unusual behavior. The other senior officers had noticed it, too.

Moylan asked, "You ever seen him like that before?"

Weir responded, "Me, never. What about it, Yates? What say you, Keogh? You two were around him during the war."

"He's fine," Yates said. "The general has been in plenty of tight spots and always gotten us through them."

"What do you think, Keogh?" asked French.

They're right about the general's behavior.

The change was unsettling, it was as if the general was asking his men for help.

Let the talk settle down.

Keogh noticed Tom Custer watching, his eyes shifting between them and the general. When the general entered his tent, Tom moved away from the group.

Those who remained received no reply from Keogh. Slowly, they started back to their respective companies.

Without saying a word, Tom motioned for Keogh to follow him away from the vicinity of the general's tent. Keogh waited until all the officers were gone.

"Thank you, for not addressing their concerns. My brother is good. I just wish he---"

"What's bothering you and Cooke so much, Tom?"

"What bothers me, Keogh, is that the scouts all agree the trails we are following are not diverging. They're going in the same direction. They keep warning the general. This could be one damn big village, with more warriors than we can handle."

141

"I think all of us are thinking along those lines. We're just hoping to catch them by surprise."

"Keogh, I need a favor from you." He held Keogh's gaze. "Since I'm riding with my brother, will you look after my C Company, please? I'll do my best to keep them close to your company. Harrington is a good man and a good officer. The company's sergeants are strong. I just have many new recruits, with no fighting experience."

"I'll do what I can, Tom."

"If you get the chance, will you talk to Cooke for me? He's more nervous than I am. You know, he mentioned something about a woman he knew from way back. First time Cooke ever mentioned a woman to me after all our years together."

So, that's part of what's bothering him.

"Keogh, did you hear what I said?"

"Yes, I will talk to Cooke."

Ten
23 June 1876

"Command, move out."

The order had been given and then passed to each company. Slowly, the tired horses of the Seventh Cavalry began trudging along. Men and horses, both caked in dust, began another day on the trail. Keogh looked at his pocket watch, five in the morning. It was cool, but all could feel the heat coming on.

He turned to look back at his I Company. He raised his right hand and motioned the troop forward. I Company was on the right flank of the Seventh Cavalry's huge column as they snaked along in the early morning light. Varden rode up next to him.

"Everyone moving, sergeant?"

"Yes, captain. Man and beast coming right along, so far. Thought you'd like to know that Captain Benteen's company was the last to report this morning. Benteen is pissed, and I mean hot. They haven't even moved out back there, yet."

"Thank you, sergeant."

~

It was late in the afternoon when Keogh made up his mind to find Cooke. Throughout the day the Seventh had come upon some deserted campsites. After the third one was found and the trail picked up, he pulled Paddy away from I Company. He let the horse stretch his legs and galloped past the other companies to catch up with the Seventh's regimental headquarters unit. He hoped to find Cooke alone.

They closed the distance behind the headquarters unit and Keogh spotted the lieutenant by himself. He pulled Paddy to a trot and moved close. Cooke never looked at him as they rode side by side.

"What in the hell are you doing out here, Keogh?"

"Just thought I'd do some catching up with an old friend, Cookie."

Neither man said a word for the next few minutes. Both watched the scouts and the general at the head of the regiment.

"You're a damn fool to be out here."

"Why do you say that? What's got you so damn rattled these days?"

After a long silence, Cooke asked, "Keogh, what in the hell do we got to show for all these years out here?"

"Well...great memories and friendship," he answered lamely. "Lots of stories and adventures, I guess."

"All those are fine," Cooke pulled his horse up and glared at him---"But they don't keep a man warm at night. They don't keep a man from dying of loneliness when the damn night won't end, now will they?"

Keogh shook his head. "Cookie, I've never heard you talk like this---are you okay?"

"I used to think I was invincible during the war. You remember how it was back in those days?"

"Yes, I do. Sometimes, I long for those days. Those memories and friends still haunt me."

"Keogh, the general has asked for help, but he's not listening to anyone. Reynolds has tried to tell him. This Boyer fellow has tried. Now, you got the Crow, Gerard and Herendeen telling him. All the signs point to one damn big village."

"Yes, well, I do feel a little apprehensive myself. With this bunch of fellows we got riding with us, on some worn out horses. Don't exactly put a man's mind at ease."

Nothing was spoken for the longest time. Both just kept on riding, lost in their thoughts.

"I never told any man what I am about to tell. You know I

come from Canada?"

"Of course I do, Cookie."

"When I was sixteen, I was madly in love with a girl back home. To this day, I still am."

"What happened?"

"Her family wasn't what my family had hoped they would be, but I didn't care. We were in love, and we had a child. When my father found out, he asked me if I still wanted to be a soldier. Being naïve of my situation, I answered in the affirmative. I soon found myself sent off to the states for schooling."

"What about the girl and your child?"

"My cousin told me my family paid her relations off. When I found out, I left school and enlisted for the Union. I did everything I could to get myself killed so I wouldn't have to live with myself and the memory of what might have been."

"I'm so sorry."

"Now, here we are. I got nothing and no one. You shouldn't be out here with us, not when you got that woman back in New York waiting for you."

"I'm going back for her when this is all over, Cookie. You can come back that way, too."

Cooke turned in his saddle and starred at him angrily. "Goddamn you, Keogh! I ought to shoot you in the damn foot right now and be done with you. Do you realize, in the next couple of days there's a good chance a great many of us won't be going home?"

The outburst startled Keogh. Everyone, it seemed, felt the same way. The Seventh was in for a rough time. Death, for many, was close. Keogh could feel it. He tried to hide his feelings as the two continued on.

Cooke gazed ahead, face blank. "Got you thinking, don't it?"

"Death and I have danced before. I don't run from it, or anything else."

Cooke shrugged. "That's good, Keogh. That's good. No man

should go to his death with any regrets."

Keogh glanced at his watch. "Almost four. I guess we've traveled thirty miles or more today." He caught a glimpse of Cooke as the lieutenant rode with his eyes closed.

Cooke pulled off his hat. With his eyes still closed, he ran his hand over his head and down his neck. "Keogh, thanks for listening to me. I've not been myself lately. I asked my cousin some time ago to find her. Wouldn't you know, she went off and got herself married."

Keogh pulled Paddy closer. "Everything will be alright, Cookie. I promise."

"I hope to God you're right. I got to get back to the rear of the column now, to find Benteen and the pack train." A smile flashed across Cooke's face. For a moment, he looked as if he had forgotten his worries. "I have to give the general a report on their progress. That is, if I can find them."

Cooke pulled his white stallion to the right and moved away. No one seemed to notice or care. Keogh watched his friend ride to the back of the column, then disappear in pursuit of the pack train. The conversation had left him wandering and sad for his friend.

All these years out here and he has no one. Christ almighty, Keogh. Nelly.

Eleven
24 June 1876

The early morning hours were already hot as the Seventh moved along the Rosebud. Hemmed in on one side by bluffs, the river had patches of timber along its banks for much of it. The country was rough, broken and dry. To cut down on the dust they produced, the Seventh moved in two parallel columns of fours. Benteen and his H Company, along with two other companies, were again in charge of the pack train.

For the first time on the campaign, Keogh felt tired and weak. Being in the saddle and on the move for over a month had started taking a toll on him. He felt agitated and more anxious by the hour. Especially as the companies were instructed to halt. The troopers dismounted to give their horses some relief.

"What in the hell has got us stopped now?" asked a trooper.

"How in the blazes would I know, you fool?" another replied.

"Easy, boys. Sit tight until you are told to move," warned Bustard. "Once the captain finds out, we'll get the orders."

Up ahead, at a distance of about two hundred yards, the general sat in conference with members of the regimental headquarters unit, the plainsmen and several of the Indian scouts.

Through his field glasses, Keogh attempted to see what was happening. They appeared to have come across a small, abandoned Indian campsite. The Arikara scouts searched through some tipis.

A short time later, the order to mount up came back to the companies. Keogh swung himself up onto Paddy and looked back for signs of Benteen. Concerned with the barely-crawling pack train, he glanced at his pocket watch.

Thirty minutes and still no Benteen. What'll happen when we strike a village?

The Seventh moved out as the Arikara scouts went to work

tearing down the tipis.

By one o'clock, the order to dismount was given. There was still no sign of Benteen and the pack train. Keogh was exhausted. He had to get some sleep, convinced it would not be long before the Indian village was found.

~

"Captain. Oh, captain, wake up," said DeRudio.

Keogh opened his eyes to see the lieutenant, Porter and Varden standing next to him. After the command had stopped, he'd fallen asleep and into a dream of Nelly. Now, though, sweat from the heat coated him, his eyes burning from the dust and lack of sleep. "What gives me the pleasure of seeing you three?"

"I was just about to make my way back to my own company, when Lieutenant Cooke caught up with me and told me what the Crow scouts found," said DeRudio. "Cooke wanted me to tell you. So, here I am."

"Well, for Christ's sake man, tell me."

"Oh, yes, about that. Seems the Crows found a big, fresh campsite over on the Rosebud, where it forks. They told the general one big village can't be far away now. The regiment is to be ready to move out by five o'clock."

"What about Benteen? Is he in yet?" Keogh asked.

"Yes, captain. They're in, but they've not had much rest," said Porter.

"First Sergeant Varden," Keogh said. "Get the company ready to move out."

"Yes sir, captain."

"Porter, you and Varden better damn well make sure we don't get stuck bringing up that goddamn pack train. You two understand me?"

Twelve

The Seventh Cavalry continued through the Rosebud Valley as evening turned to night. It didn't take long to find more abandoned campsites, each one bigger than the last. All in the regiment knew they were close to finding a big village. The thought of an ambush weighed heavily on everyone's minds.

By eight o'clock in the evening, the regiment settled into camp. The Seventh Cavalry had gone twenty-eight miles over the entire day. On this night, there would be only one fire per company, and each trooper would picket his own horse. The order to move out could be given at a moment's notice.

I Company made their camp with the rest of the Seventh on the west side of the Rosebud. After attending to their horses, most of the troopers tried to get some sleep. Others sat around the fire talking, while some even went for baths in the river.

Anxious to hear what Tom and Cooke knew, Keogh stood. "Porter, I'm going over to headquarters to see Captain Custer and Lieutenant Cooke," he said. "Varden, when Captain Benteen and the pack train get in, let the captain know we've saved him a spot next to us for his command to rest."

The stifling Plains heat had finally disappeared, replaced by a cool breeze which brought much needed relief to man, horse and mule.

On his way to headquarters, Keogh ran into several of the Arikara scouts. They sat by their fires, talking, drinking coffee and smoking. Some of the scouts hummed a song, or so it seemed to him.

With them sat Reynolds. He was seated with his legs crossed over one another on the ground next to Bloody Knife. He stared straight ahead at the fire and rocked back and forth slowly. "What brings you this way, Keogh?" he asked.

"Just heading over to headquarters to get the latest."

Reynolds relayed his talk with Keogh to Bloody Knife using sign language. "Bloody Knife says the general isn't listening. The general is so worried we might miss a trail, he doesn't grasp the meaning of all of them."

"What in the hell do you mean?"

Agitated, Reynolds rose to his feet. "What I mean, and what all of us are trying to tell you soldier boys, including the general, is that these Indians are not leaving. They are all meeting up to form one big village. They know we're coming, and they don't care, Keogh! Somebody around here better get the general to figure it out, and I mean in a hurry! We might just get into a mess we can't get out of!" He relayed more of the conversation to Bloody Knife and the Arikara nodded in agreement.

"Then why don't you two come with me? We'll tell this to Captain Custer and Lieutenant Cooke. They'll pass it on to the general."

"He's not listening to anyone, Keogh, but we will come along."

~

At the headquarters campsite, a flurry of activity greeted them. The Crow had just returned from scouting further to the west. All in attendance listened as Boyer relayed their findings to the general. Kellogg was especially interested and took notes. He hoped it would be something he could use in a story. Cooke, Tom, Sharrow, Gerard, Herendeen, Dorman and the general's striker, Private John Burkman, were there. Two privates from C Company stood watch as bodyguards for the general this night. Two trumpeters stood close if needed.

"General, the Crow say they returned from a lookout where they hide out on raids against the Cheyenne and Sioux in this area," Boyer said. "They say, from that vantage point, you can see the entire valley below, toward the Little Bighorn to the west. The hostile's trail leads that direction. If there are Indians on the Little Bighorn, we should be able to see them in the morning."

Lieutenant Varnum joined the meeting, brought by Chief Trumpeter Voss.

"Well, Varnum, I can see by your condition you're having a rough time of it. Voss, get me Lieutenant Hare," ordered the general.

"I can do whatever task you present me with, sir," Varnum replied.

"Good. I want you to accompany the Crow with Boyer and go to this lookout. Take a couple of Arikara as messengers and report back. Take Reynolds with you as well. I want to make sure we get the lay of the land."

The lieutenant looked at the plainsman. "Are you up to it?"

Reynolds laughed. "I can go anywhere you go, soldier boy."

"See that it gets done," the general ordered. "Lieutenant Cooke, officers' call at nine-thirty."

Keogh hastened back to I Company, hoping to find Benteen had made it in with the pack train. As he approached the campfire, familiar voices reached his ears. He moved closer, relieved to see Benteen. The captain lay next to the small fire, his boots off and his hat over face. DeRudio was telling stories again.

"There I was, a prisoner on the infamous Devil's Island!" said DeRudio. "I said to myself, DeRudio, you're done for!"

"Oh, Jesus Christ, man, here we go again," muttered Benteen from beneath his hat. "DeRudio, do you expect us to believe you were a prisoner on Devil's Island? Count No Account on Devil's Island? I doubt it very much."

"It is a known fact, captain."

Benteen removed the hat from his face. "The only fact I know is that I'm damn tired." The captain shut his eyes and rolled to his side. "I have a premonition we won't be staying here too long."

Keogh moved into the fire's light.

"Any news for us?" asked Moylan.

Benteen sat up. "Bully for you, Keogh. Thanks for holding me and my company a spot to skip off on. I'm your man."

"Yes, I have some news. As we speak, the Crows are headed back to a lookout where they can see into the valley of the Little Bighorn. From the direction the trails are heading, they think the hostiles might be there. The general has ordered an officers' call at nine-thirty."

"What say you now, Benteen?" asked McDougall. "Do you think we'll be on the move tonight?"

"Surely to God not," Moylan said. "It's pitch black in this camp, not to mention how dark it would be stumbling around if we moved again. We're liable to run right into a mess of them out there."

"Moylan, when are you going to learn?" scolded Benteen. "The best time to hit an Indian village is in the wee hours of the morning. So, unless they're right over yonder, we'll be on the jump."

Thirteen

Outside the general's tent sat Lieutenant Wallace at a small table. Cooke held a lantern for him as he made notations on a map. Sharrow waited close.

Keogh stood next to Benteen. He and the captain were quiet as the officers talked among themselves. The two had not shared a word to any of the others concerning their apprehension with the general and his intentions to complete the mission, regardless the obstacles.

Sergeant Major Sharrow cracked the heels of his boots together. The general and Tom exited the tent.

"At ease, gentlemen," ordered the general. He was hatless and the sleeves to his blue fireman shirt were rolled up. "The reason I have called you all here is this, our Crow scouts brought back word from a lookout on a divide between the Rosebud and Little Bighorn valleys. From there, they can see west toward the Little Bighorn River. It would appear the hostiles could be on the river."

The officers looked at one another in excitement. Keogh could sense and see the cautious optimism on their faces.

"The regiment will move out at twenty-two hundred hours tonight. We will cross the divide and conceal ourselves during the day for some much needed rest. We will reconnoiter the valley to be sure of the hostiles' location and village size," said the general. "We will hit them on the morning of the twenty-sixth!"

~

By the time Keogh arrived at the I Company campsite, word that the Seventh was to move out had already reached his men. To his dismay, disorder and confusion had set in.

I should have issued orders to get the company ready in case we moved out.

Very dumb, Keogh.

Since Benteen's H Company had camped close, the troopers of both companies became mixed up. Adding to the chaos, was the fact that both company's horses were picketed in close proximity to one another. It didn't help matters that I Company's dog, Joe, was raising hell with the pack train's mules. Troopers stumbled, cursed, and crowded each other trying to make their way to their horses in the dark. Mules brayed and kicked as Joe barked.

It was almost too much for Keogh to take.

Pack train and mules. Goddamn pack train, after all these years out here. This is what it comes to?

"Get me some order in here, Varden! Damn it to hell!" His commands went unheard. "Where the hell is my orderly and trumpeter?"

Quickly, I Company's two trumpeters, Patton and McGucker appeared. Gustave Korn, Keogh's orderly, followed. Keogh wanted to have a bugle blown, anything to get some order to the situation.

"McGucker get your ass over there and find the company. Tell the sergeants to get some order restored, and I mean now! Korn, get Paddy saddled. Patton, stay close." Keogh wheeled around just in time to see Benteen's orderly hurrying off to report H Company was ready.

Damn Benteen. I should have listened to him. He knew we'd move out tonight.

154

Fourteen

The Seventh Cavalry was back on the trail, moving along a creek, headed west. In the darkness, they trudged over the rough and broken terrain, the only sounds from the horses' hooves hitting the ground and the jangle of the gear strapped to them.

The only way for Keogh to be sure they were headed in the right direction was to follow the echo of clinking tin cups from the company ahead. The distance seemed to be growing larger between the regiment and his I Company as they escorted the pack train.

Keogh pulled Paddy off to the side to wait on his company.

"Captain, Joe here wants to say he is sorry for causing so much hell back yonder," said I Company guidon carrier, Private O'Bryan. The dog sat on O'Bryan's lap as they rode behind Keogh with Trumpeter Patton and Korn.

The tough little dog knew he was in trouble and he whimpered for Keogh to pet him, wagging his tail slightly. After some time, Keogh leaned over and patted the dog's head.

It had been a rough and exhausting night escorting the pack train. To compound matters, it was pitch black even with the stars shinning. Keogh's anger had subsided for the moment. He checked his pocket watch.

One in the morning. What's done is done. Keep your head about you.

"Captain, the packers and troopers are having a rough time back there," said DeLacy. The sergeant had been sent from the pack train to find Keogh. "F Company is having a hell of a time getting the mules to move and keeping the packs on them. How much longer are we going to stumble through this damn dark night?"

"Sergeant DeLacy, get back there, and you tell Porter and Mathey that if I have to come back there, it's going to get damn uncomfortable for all parties involved."

"Yes, captain." The sergeant swung his bay horse around and headed back to the sound of the pack train. To find his way, all he had to do was follow the cursing of the troopers trying to guide the cantankerous mules.

Keogh dismounted Paddy. Smart enough to know that, when at a standstill, you gave your horse some relief, the troopers riding with him followed his lead.

"Captain Keogh," DeRudio said. "I found you, captain."

"What in the hell is it, DeRudio?"

"Captain Custer sent me back to hurry you on the trail."

DeRudio was accompanied by a trumpeter. Both turned and reached for their revolvers at every noise. Their eyes darted to the sounds of the oncoming pack train, then shifted back on the trail they'd just traveled.

"What's got you two looking so spooked?" asked Keogh. "We thought for sure that we might find Indians between the regiment and you back here, that's all," DeRudio replied.

"Well, you found us. Now get yourselves to Captain Custer and have them stop, before Indians do find us."

~

It was three o'clock in the morning when Keogh and I Company fell into the Seventh Cavalry's campsite. He reasoned his I Company had been a good hour behind the rest of the regiment. He was thankful the regiment had stopped and allowed them to catch up. Men and horses were weary. Most troopers dropped to the ground and picketed their horses next to them, too tired and exhausted to do anything else.

Korn took hold of Paddy and Keogh threw himself onto the ground to rest.

"If you ever find yourself in a bad way out there---and I mean so bad that, no matter how hard you try, it's not going to work---you let Comanche carry you

156

away and don't look back. Don't you look back! Just the two of you run back here to me. Don't you try to save all of them from going to hell, you hear me? You have nothing to prove to any man, Myles Keogh. You have fought and done enough in your lifetime. Your soul needs to rest. Please, Myles, please!"

I promise, Nelly. I promise.

"Wake up, Keogh," said Tom.

Keogh opened his eyes. "What's going on? What time is it?"

"Everything is fine for now. We just came back this way to see if you'd made it into camp. Mathey told us you all had a hell of a time with the mules last night," Tom said.

"He's right," said Keogh. "We had to cut several packs loose. I was under orders from the general not to fall too far behind. Any news on the trail?"

"The general got word from Varnum to come on for a look. He just left with Gerard and Bloody Knife," Tom said. "We're to move out in one hour."

"What about the packs on the back trail?" Keogh asked.

"I'll have Yates send a detail from his company to get them."

Fifteen
25 June 1876
One mile from lookout between
Rosebud and Little Bighorn Valley

After a few precious hours of rest, the Seventh moved on. Keogh and his I Company were still escorting the pack train when the regiment stopped in a ravine surrounded by hills. Clusters of pine and juniper trees dotted the landscape. Sagebrush covered the ground.

"Captain Keogh, Captain Keogh!" hollered Sergeant Curtis.

The burly sergeant from F Company and four of his troopers pulled up their horses. The F Company detail had their revolvers drawn, their horses lathered in sweat.

"What is it, sergeant?"

"Captain, we ran into Indians on the back trail when we went back for the packs!"

"Did they see you?"

"Yes, captain, they saw us. We fired on them, but they got away. They got to know we're out here!"

There was only one thing to do now. Keogh knew he had to alert Tom that the regiment had been discovered. "Porter, stay here with the company and pack train. I'm going ahead to find Captain Custer."

The regiment was still stopped as Keogh made his way forward. As he approached the headquarters unit, Calhoun and Yates pulled away from their companies and followed. Tom and Cooke watched the three ride up.

"Tom, we've been spotted by Indians on the back trail!" said Keogh.

"Are you sure?" he asked.

"The detail Yates sent back ran into a party of Indians going through the packs. It's a good bet they're letting the village know we're out here."

Calhoun said, "Here comes the general and Gerard."

"Come on," said Tom.

"Ho, Vic," the general said to his horse. He pointed at the command, then let the horse move sideways, back into a trot past Tom and Calhoun.

Gerard said, "Boyer and Reynolds got him convinced the Sioux have us under watch and are letting the village know about us now. They spotted some lurking to the west. Varnum saw seven of them to the north as well. The Crow want him to attack immediately!"

The general pulled his horse up by the headquarters unit. "Voss, soft officers call," he ordered.

~

"Gentlemen, the day to attack is at hand," said General Custer. "The scouts and Mr. Boyer have seen indications that would lead them to believe we have found an Indian village. The village is some fifteen miles from here, on the Little Bighorn River. Furthermore, the regiment has been discovered. Time is of the essence. We will move out immediately, find the village, and attack!"

Keogh looked around the group assembled. He could sense the apprehension, see the worry in their eyes.

This is what we came to do. Find the village and drive the Indians to the reservations. The hour is at hand.

His thoughts were jarred by the worried words and tone of the scouts and plainsmen riding with the regiment. They all tried to warn the general of just how great an undertaking they were about to attempt.

"I am to leave you now, general," Herendeen said. "I ask permission to rendezvous with General Terry and Gibbon's command now."

"There is no need for you to go," said the general. "It is of no use now, as the Indians are in our front. Besides, I need you here with me."

"That has got to be the biggest gathering of Plains Indians, maybe ever. Just waiting for us," Reynold said.

The general said nothing, just stared ahead with a blank look in his eyes.

Boyer continued to voice the warning. "There are more Indians out there than we can handle all alone. We get out there and walk into them, we're all liable to wake up in hell!"

"You all are not soldiers. You are not required to go with the regiment," General Custer said.

"You know damn well I'm going Custer," said a terse Reynolds.

Dorman said, "I'm going, no matter what."

"We have come this far with you," Gerard said. "No use in turning back now."

The general had more orders. "Each troop commander shall assign one non-commissioned officer and six troopers to the pack train to protect it. We will move out immediately to attack. The last company commander to report back with their company's readiness will have the honor to bring up the pack train. Your company will march in the order of who reports first. I want each troop to resupply their ammunition as well."

The officers turned and began to head back to their respective companies. No one wanted to be left out of the fight, stuck bringing up the pack train. No sooner had the general dismissed the officers, then Benteen said, "H Company is ready and reporting for duty, general."

The general was clearly caught off guard. Every officer stopped and looked back at him. "The advance is yours, Captain Benteen."

Determined not to get stuck with the pack train again, Keogh moved quickly. When he reached his company, it dawned on him that Captain McDougall had not been at the briefing.

I got him.

Sixteen

"First Sergeant Varden," Keogh said. "Assemble the company, on the double."

"You heard the captain, fall in!" ordered Varden.

"Korn, saddle Comanche for me," Keogh ordered.

The men of I Company jumped to their feet and moved into formation. They were dirty, their uniforms caked in dust after being out in the field for over a month. Most were in need of a haircut and a shave. Many a trooper's pants showed holes and were covered in stains. They fell in and stood at attention.

"I Company, the hour is at hand. We are moving out on the double to attack the village," Keogh said. "Do not be afraid. Do what we order you to do and we will get through it." He eyed the men standing before him. "I will command first platoon with First Sergeant Varden. Lieutenant Porter will have second platoon with Sergeant Bustard. Sergeant Delacy will take six troopers and head back to the pack train to be part of its escort. When the word comes, you're not going to have time to do anything except attack and try to survive. We're hitting a damn big village up ahead. So, check your saddles and make yourselves ready. It's going to be a long and hot day."

In a matter of minutes, I Company was ready. Each trooper stood next to his horse, in formation, and waited for the order to mount up.

Next to Comanche, Keogh waited. Korn, Patton and O'Bryan stood close. The company's guidon fluttered from the breeze of the late morning. It was already beginning to heat up as the sun shone down on the regiment as Keogh watched the flurry of activity.

Up ahead and out in front of the Seventh Cavalry, sat the general atop his mare. He was busy talking to Cooke and Tom. Now and then, a scout would ride up and converse with the group.

Varnum and the Arikara and Sioux scouts were posted off ahead and to the regiment's left. They'd been instructed to run off the Indian village's pony herd when it was found. As the Arikara awaited the order to move out, they applied a mud mixture to their bodies. It had been brought from their native grounds, back on the Missouri River. They believed the mixture would protect them in battle.

Lastly, to the regiment's right, were Boyer, four Crow scouts, Lieutenant Hare and a few Arikara. Close to this group sat Dorman, Cross and Jackson. Herendeen, Gerard and Reynolds ranged up ahead, riding to and from the general's position. Then, the word came back.

"Mount up!"

The scouts fanned out and took the lead on both sides. When they had gone a short distance, the general started his advance with two Crow scouts. The regimental headquarters unit followed, with Benteen's H Company leading the main column.

I Company had just begun to move out when they heard the familiar bark of Joe. Keogh had ordered the men to leave the little dog back with the pack train and, if need be, tied up.

His order had been disobeyed.

Joe barked at the men left to guard the pack train. Captain McDougall and his B Company sat close and watched. Joe seemed to relish the attention as he barked at General Custer's orderly, Burkman. The orderly held the general's dogs to keep them from following.

~

It was a little past noon when the regiment stopped. They'd crossed a divide between two creeks, with the huge Indian trail easy to see as it ran toward the Little Bighorn River.

Keogh dismounted Comanche and checked his saddle. He made sure the two revolvers he'd strapped on each side to the front of the saddle were fully loaded. From his time in the war, he'd learned you could never have too many revolvers when fighting from atop a horse.

Up ahead, he watched the general out front with Cooke. The lieutenant wrote notes in his field notebook, then pulled his horse to the right to deliver instructions. Boyer and one of the Crow accompanied the general. The three had a lively conversation until the general suddenly pulled his horse away dismissively.

Too hot to keep his buckskin jacket on now, Keogh removed it, folded it up and tied it to the back of Comanche's saddle. He rolled the sleeves of his blue fireman shirt as well. He then felt for his Angus Dei necklace under his shirt. He closed his eyes and said a silent prayer.

Next, Keogh checked his Winchester sporting rifle and put it back into the scabbard on Comanche. He pulled both revolvers from the canvas belt around his waist and checked to make sure both were loaded.

With his revolvers ready and knife firmly in its scabbard, there was nothing left to do. He was as ready as he would ever be for what lay ahead. He took a big drink from his canteen, then poured a little of the water on a red kerchief and wiped the inside of his wide brimmed field hat, then wrapped the kerchief loosely around his neck.

Cooke rode back past the companies until he found Keogh. "The general is ordering Benteen and three companies to the bluffs to the left. You are to follow the general along the creek with your company and companies C, E, F and L. Reno will follow to the left with three companies."

Captain Benteen and his Company H, followed by Companies D and K, moved to the left of the creek that the Seventh followed. The captain then swung his command to the west. Benteen's job was to check for scattered Indian camps suspected to be on the smaller creeks in the valley of the Little Bighorn River.

General Custer raised himself out of the saddle and waved his hat at Benteen's command. Keogh watched the captain--- nothing. He was sure by Benteen's refusal to acknowledge the general that the captain was not happy about his mission.

That's what I was afraid of. I knew eventually something would happen between the two of them.

Seventeen

General Custer and the five companies he commanded continued following the Indian trail. Out ahead of the companies, the
scouts surveyed the huge lodge pole and travois trail along the
creek. Behind came Yates and F Company, Company E being led
by Smith, Calhoun and his L Company, Keogh and I Company,
and C Company led by Harrington.

Reno's battalion crossed the creek and now rode parallel to the
five companies General Custer led. With Reno were companies A,
G and M. The pack train, led by Mathey and escorted by Mc-
Dougall's B Company, had already fallen out of sight.

Keogh studied his pocket watch. It was twelve-thirty. Benteen's
battalion had moved away from the main column of the Seventh,
and he could no longer see them.

The Seventh pressed on along the creek for twenty minutes. A
lone figure then cut out from the headquarters unit. Keogh strained
his eyes to catch a glimpse of the solitary silhouette headed to the
left. He figured it might be a messenger for Benteen. After sometime, he was able to recognize Voss, the Seventh's Chief Trumpeter.

~

For the next hour and a half, the Seventh Cavalry continued
down the Indian trail along the creek. Scattered groves of cottonwood and box elder lined the banks. The heat had risen, growing
even stronger, and most troopers had taken off their blue wool
Army jackets by now. Some wore gray shirts, some wore faded blue
shirts and some even sported gingham shirts. Men and horses were
thirsty and tired, but still motivated by the promised chance of big
adventure with fame.

The general, with two Crow scouts and the headquarters unit close, moved at a brisk walk. When the terrain allowed, they moved at a trot.

Reno and his battalion continued to ride parallel to the five companies across the creek from them. At times, they fell from one hundred to three hundred yards behind.

The column stopped. Off to the side of I Company, Keogh pulled Comanche from the group, joined by his orderly, Korn. Keogh noticed a commotion ahead. He removed his field glasses and, watched the Crow scouts as they moved around two tipis. He could make out Hare, Herendeen and Boyer. The group waved the general up the hill.

The headquarters unit had stopped in the vicinity of the tipis. Keogh watched the general, Gerard and Bloody Knife in conversation. Kellogg, the newspaperman, had caught up to the group and was scribbling notes. In a matter of minutes, Cooke moved back to the headquarters unit with Hare.

From there, a rider moved away and rode toward Reno. The major and his three companies had now crossed over to the right side of the creek. As they moved, they passed the five companies.

Keogh turned his field glasses back in the vicinity of where the general sat. Several different Indian scouts were coming and going, and two of the Crow moved down the creek toward the Little Bighorn River. Varnum rode to the general's position with some Arikara scouts.

With a wave of his hat, General Custer motioned Tom to bring the Seventh up close to the tipis. Keogh continued on with Korn, staying to the right of I Company. Cooke rode in their direction. "What say you, Cookie?" asked Keogh.

"Come on, Keogh. I need you to go with me to give Reno some courage," he said.

"Go back to the company. Tell Lieutenant Porter the command is his. Stay with him," ordered Keogh.

"Yes, captain," said Korn.

Keogh swung Comanche around to approach Reno's battalion. "What's got you looking so worried?" he asked.

"The general is splitting us up without knowing just where the village is," said Cooke. "I don't like it."

Reno and his adjutant, Hodgson, came riding toward the pair.

"What do you supposed Custer intends to do?" asked Keogh.

"I don't think he knows just yet," replied Cooke. "That's what's bothering me."

The major and Hodgson pulled their horses up. "What are my orders, Cooke?" Reno asked.

"Major, there are Indians up ahead watching us as we speak. The scouts have seen groups of them fleeing. You are to take your command as fast as you think proper and charge them, wherever you may find them. We will support you. Take the scouts with you," said Cooke.

Reno and Hodgson turned their horses and let them trot for the head of the three companies. The major formed his command in columns of two and moved for the river. Ahead of Reno rode the Arikara scouts and a detail of ten troopers from M Company, led by Hare. Keogh and Cooke followed.

Eighteen
The Little Bighorn River

Major Reno's battalion crossed back to the left side of the creek and rode for half an hour before the Little Bighorn River appeared.

"Command forward," ordered Reno. "Once we cross, pass the word we will reform on the other side, Hodgson."

"Yes, sir," replied the lieutenant.

It was not a well-organized crossing for Reno and his command. Several of the troopers stopped to water their horses in the middle of the river, while others seemed hell bent on getting to the other side as quickly as they could.

At the crossing, Keogh and Cooke watched from a knoll. Cooke shook his head and hollered, "For God's sake, men, don't run those horses like that! You'll need them very shortly!"

It was to no avail. For many of these troopers, this was their first time out atop a horse, let alone in combat. Their emotions were high and the horses could feel it. As the last of Reno's three companies crossed, Lieutenants Varnum and Wallace rode up.

"What in the hell are you doing with this group, Varnum?" asked Cooke.

"The general said we could come along with Reno, to get in on the action," replied Varnum.

Reno crossed the river with Hodgson. On the other side, Captains French and Moylan along with Lieutenant DeRudio, tried to get the companies into some sort of fighting formation. With the three companies rode Reynolds, Gerard, Dorman, and Herendeen, along with scouts Jackson and Cross. A couple of the Crow had come along as well.

"I am heading back to the regiment, Cookie. You coming?" Keogh asked.

"Go on. I'm going to watch Reno to see that he gets them in order to make a charge," Cooke said. "By the time you and the regiment get close, I might still be here."

Towards the rising dust column of the Seventh Cavalry Keogh turned Comanche. He desperately wanted to get back to his I Company before they attacked the Indian village. It didn't take long until the five companies came into view. The general and Tom rode ahead.

"What's going on up ahead with Reno?" asked General Custer.

"When I left him a short time ago, he was forming his men to charge," Keogh said.

"Hold up, Keogh!" Cooke hollered. The lieutenant pulled up his white stallion, dismounted and removed his buckskin jacket. "Reno is charging the village down in the valley. General, Gerard came back and told me to tell you the Indians are not running, but coming out to fight!"

General Custer turned and waved the Seventh up to his position. Yates and his F Company were in front. "Captain Yates, take the companies down the valley and water the horses," ordered General Custer.

~

After a short pause to water the horses, the five companies and the general fell back into formation. They were about to cross the river in support of Reno and his three companies when several in the unit noticed an Indian trail diverging. The trail ran to the right and went up the bluffs to the northeast.

Tom came riding back to the headquarters units' position. "General, hold up."

"What is it, Tom?" General Custer asked.

"I have been told there are warriors on the bluffs. Look to the northeast of us," Tom said, then dismounted his horse and pointed.

Mitch Boyer was stopped and sat with some of the Crow scouts on the bluffs above the Little Bighorn River. To their right, one hundred yards east of them, was a squad from F Company, acting as advance flankers for the regiment. To the north of both groups sat what appeared to be mounted Indian warriors.

"Varnum had said the valley was full of warriors. The village must still be standing. They're trying to buy some time for the women and children to move," said General Custer. "Any word from Benteen yet?"

"He has not reported, general," Cooke said.

"We'll hit them on their flank while Reno has the warriors occupied," announced the general. He pulled his horse in the direction of the bluffs. "Command, move out."

Nineteen
The Bluffs

For the bluffs the Seventh moved. It was a gradual climb, and once completed, the terrain turned to rolling hills. The dust and afternoon heat pressed down on the command.

Lieutenant Riley and the F Company squad he led waved the Seventh on.

The five companies fell into a slow trot, now riding abreast in columns of two, moving onto the crest of the hill toward where the F Company squad set. It was here the Indian warriors had last been seen.

The hill at the top was an expansive area, with a depression in the middle. When Keogh and his I Company were almost to it, he could see the general, Tom, Yates, Cooke, and the general's nephew, Autie Reed, looking out over the vast valley floor. He pulled Comanche away from I Company for a better look.

The valley stretched out before the command some three hundred feet below. The ground toward the river consisted of a series of ravines and gullies. They were everywhere… deep, wide and sinister looking. They would be hard to maneuver if one had to take a horse through.

Reno's battalion advanced across the valley. The river and some timber were to their right. Ahead of them, to their left and west, the Arikara scouts moved for an immense pony herd.

Behind Keogh, the five companies passed. Excited troopers hollered, while others had trouble controlling their horses. Several pulled out of the column to control their excited mounts.

"Hold your horses, boys!" hollered the general. "There are enough Indians down there for all of us."

Captain Yates took the lead and moved the command further to the northeast. They moved at a trot, over the rolling hills of grassland overlooking the Little Bighorn River.

The general and the headquarters unit continued to survey the valley. Boyer and four Crow scouts moved ahead, along the bluffs. A half a mile away to the northeast, the F Company squad advanced with Riley.

Keogh pulled Comanche up and to the left, his company continued on and thundered past the two of them, following the rest in the battalion. He lifted his field glasses and looked to the south in hopes of seeing Benteen or McDougall. He saw neither.

General Custer, though, had seen enough. He now led the headquarters unit as they followed Boyer and the Crow scouts along the bluffs above the river. Kellogg, atop his mule tried to keep up. To their right, riding parallel to them, came the five companies, riding abreast in columns of two. After going three fourths of a mile, the headquarters unit stopped.

The general, Tom, Cooke, an orderly trumpeter, Boyer, and the Crow scouts were now on a part of the bluffs that extended out and above the river. The position gave them a commanding view of the valley below and Reno's battalion as it advanced.

To Reno's front, the beginnings of an Indian village was clearly visible. Peering into the valley below, the clarity of what was happening was seen by all.

The Indian village spread before them. Dust clouds to the northwest of the village indicated people in flight. They'd been taken by surprise. The pony herd to the west of the village was being driven to the north while, small groups of mounted warriors rode for Reno's advancing battalion. Others chased after Arikara scouts and the stolen ponies. None seemed to notice the general's command on the bluffs. The moment was not lost on the passing Seventh Cavalry troopers.

"Reno is charging them!" said one excited trooper to no one in particular.

Another trooper exclaimed, "You can see the village. It looks huge!"

"We need to get down there before the fight is over," another trooper said.

Keogh made his way to the group on the edge of the bluffs. He again scanned the valley with his field glasses. His stomach stirred uneasy at what he saw.

The immense valley held an Indian village that looked like it went on for a mile, or more. Trees, the course of the land, and the river blocked part of the view. South of the village, Reno's battalion continued to close in.

The Crow scouts used sign language with Boyer in an effort to communicate with the general.

"What are they saying, Boyer?" asked Cooke.

Kellogg readied his pencil. Sure whatever was said next, could be a big story.

"They want you to go back down into the valley and follow Reno. They say we will run right through them if we follow Reno."

"No," said General Custer. He lowered his field glasses. "There will be enough fighting for us later. Let Reno fight down there."

The Crow scouts waited for Boyer's response, and Keogh watched them shake their heads in confusion. He was concerned at what he just heard. The general had promised to support Reno, yet, here they were, in no position to do so.

Kellogg scratched his head with his pencil, hoping for more.

Keogh turned his field glasses back toward Reno's command. More warriors swarmed toward them. Now, he was very worried. He knew the major wouldn't be able to continue the attack.

Reno doesn't have enough men!

Cooke said, "General, look south. It must be Benteen and the pack train. Looks like they're on the trail and following."

With his field glasses, Keogh looked back at the trail the five companies had traveled. He hoped to see Benteen or the pack train. Neither were visible, but two separate dust clouds seemed to be coming into the valley.

Thank God!

"Boyer," said General Custer. "How far to the nearest crossing where we can hit the village?"

"A little less than two miles. There is a coulee the tribes have been using for years to get to the river. It could be a little rough crossing there," he answered.

Keogh wheeled to head for I Company. Once there, he was met by Porter and Varden. Before he could speak, loud cheering erupted from the men of the five companies. The troopers in the Seventh Cavalry watched General Custer wave his hat at them as he rode past.

"Courage, men, courage!" shouted the general. "We've caught them napping, boys."

The general and his orderly trumpeter rode up a sloping hill for a better vantage point. There, General Custer trained his field glasses on the valley below. At the same time, Tom and Cooke moved in the direction of the headquarters unit.

"Sergeant Major Sharrow!" Tom hollered. "Get me Finckle up here on the double."

The Sergeant Major turned his horse and made his way to C Company's position. He arrived just in time to see C Company Sergeant August Finckle as he rode up and rejoined his company.

Finckle was no stranger to soldiering and fighting, having served in the Prussian Army. The sergeant dismounted from his horse and patted the animal's neck as he watched Sharrow come his way. The horse had had trouble keeping up with the rest of the command, laboring on the climb up the bluffs.

The C Company Sergeant was only one man of many having trouble with a horse who could not keep up with the command. Seeing the condition of Finckle's horse, Sharrow chose another C Company Sergeant.

"Go to Captain McDougall with the pack train and bring him

straight across," ordered Tom. "If any packs fall off, don't stop. If you see Captain Benteen, tell him to come on!"

Sergeant Daniel Knipe replied, "Yes, sir," and saluted. He turned his Roan Sorrel horse and rode south.

~

Their time had come. One last chance for the men to check the horses and themselves, before they faced whatever lay ahead. Many in the command had dismounted to tighten saddles and to discard any unneeded equipment that might hinder them and their horse, in the fight that was sure to come. Some troopers put away their wide brimmed hats. Others took their kerchiefs from around their necks and tied it across their foreheads.

Keogh swung up onto Comanche and turned in the saddle to look behind him to the south one last time. He saw four troopers who had fallen out of the ranks. They struggled to get their exhausted horses up and on the move. Sergeant Knipe disappeared behind them in search of Benteen and the pack train. There was no more time. He had to go. "Let's go, boy."

General Custer and the headquarters unit moved north, followed by the rest of the command trying to keep up.

Come on, Benteen. Come on!

~

Captain Benteen and the three companies he'd led had now returned to the Indian trail after their two hour reconnaissance of the valley. They had encountered no Indians and Benteen had sent no message to the general. In a matter of minutes, they came upon a morass and halted, the commands' horses had not had water since the previous day.

After watering their horses for close to thirty minutes, Benteen's command heard the lead mules of Captain McDougall's pack train coming towards them. The mules were thirsty and Benteen was savvy enough to get his command on the move again before the entire pack train arrived. On down the valley his command moved. The faint sound of gunfire could be heard. Benteen was only four miles behind General Custer and the five companies now.

~

Over the rolling hills to the north, the Seventh moved. Up ahead, along the bluffs, sat two humpbacked hills, with another to their right. The general and the headquarters unit followed the terrain to the base of the hill.

Boyer and the Crow scouts stayed to the Seventh's left, following the steep bluffs above the river, and moved on past the humpbacked hills as the general, Tom, Cooke and an orderly trumpeter dismounted and climbed. They stopped and looked out on the valley. The Indian village was now in plain sight.

Keogh dismounted near the headquarters unit at the base of the hill. All eyes were on the general as he returned. "Village appears to be scattering," said the general. "Reno advancing in skirmish line. He has the warriors fighting and occupied."

"Women, children and dogs running in all directions!" Tom said.

"We will move on down the river, cross and get them rounded up. Command, prepare to move out," ordered the general.

The Seventh advanced over the hill and found a vast and open country before them. To their left, the bluffs above the river concealed their movements. They followed the terrain as it pushed the command to the right against a series of peaks. The F Company squad moved ahead and entered a coulee, which turned the command ever so slightly to the right. They moved in columns of four now. After traveling to the northeast for some distance, they found the advance squad in another coulee and were forced to turn to the west.

Surrounded by sloping hills scorched brown, the Seventh traveled along the coulee's flat valley floor. Just on the other side, over a rise, another coulee. The coulees formed a V-shaped valley. Pockets of sagebrush dotted the landscape. To the left, stood the bluffs running parallel to the river. Behind, the ground rose to a series of hills and ridges.

The command spurred to a gallop, but only for a short time. Ahead one and a half miles lay the Little Bighorn River.

The general and some of the headquarters unit moved further to the northeast some distance. Keogh watched as they stopped on a hill, below a ridge and looked through their field glasses toward the river.

~

Back where the scouts had come upon the abandoned Indian tipis, Sergeant Knipe completed part of his mission. He'd found Captain Benteen and his three companies. "They want you up there as quick as you can," said Knipe. "They've struck a big Indian village." The sergeant never slowed his horse. He continued on past Benteen's command for the pack train.

Benteen said nothing.

Twenty
The Coulee

For what seemed like eternity, the five companies waited and watched. Their horses felt the excitement and anxiety, the tension seeping into them as they nervously pawed the ground.

"What in the hell are we waiting for now?" asked a trooper.

Another chimed in. "I want me a buffalo robe and a squaw to go with it."

"Keep quiet in the ranks!" ordered Sergeant John Ogden, E Company.

Sergeant Frederick Nursey, F Company, hollered, "Shut the hell up and listen."

All in the command listened and looked in the direction of the bluffs. The roar of gunfire echoed.

"That's got to be Reno's boys giving them hell," said a trooper. "The damn fight will be over before we get into it."

A rider hastened toward the command from the bluffs above the river. From behind him, more gunfire carried across the coulee. As he neared, Keogh recognized him. It was the scout, Boyer. The Crow scouts who had been riding with him were nowhere to be seen.

The conversation between Boyer and the general did not last long. When it was over, Sergeant Major Sharrow received orders, saluted and moved back in the direction of the five companies. He pulled his horse up by Keogh and grinned. "Captain, the general is requesting you."

Keogh's grip tightened around the reins.

Please, God, let me be given a chance. Please, Lord, please. Just this one time.

Keogh and Sharrow dismounted by the general and those in the headquarters unit.

"Captain, this is it. It's time we get into the fight," said the general. "Boyer says Reno's been stopped. Some of his command has moved off the skirmish line."

Boyer pointed. "This coulee will get you to a crossing that will put you into the village. The women and children are moving down river. It looks like all the warriors are busy with Reno. Keep your eyes open, though, there has got to be some warriors around. It's only a matter of time before they get here."

Keogh raised his field glasses to his eyes and scanned the terrain to the river.

"Captain, take your company with C and E Companies. Find us a suitable crossing, secure it and then set up a defensive perimeter," ordered the general. "Blow the charge when you get ready to cross and we will follow you. Remember, when the warriors realize our intentions, get ready to be a blocking force. Once we're all across, I will take F and L on down the river to get the women and children. If you can't find a good place to cross, stay back from the river a ways and continue looking for one. We will cover you."

"Understood, general," replied Keogh. "Thank you, sir."

"Good luck, captain," said General Custer.

Keogh urged Comanche into a trot, back to the officers who had gathered at the head of the five companies. Before he could issue orders, all had turned their attention to a soldier on a gray horse, one of the general's orderly trumpeters, Martini.

The trumpeter had been summoned by Cooke. After taking orders from the general, Cooke had written a message in his field notebook, then ripped out the sheet of paper. He handed it to the trumpeter. Martini saluted, then turned his horse in the direction of the coulee the command had just moved through.

"Yates, you and Calhoun will stay with the general. I am taking C and E to the river. Sturgis, you find us a place to cross when we get close," Keogh said. "Once across, we will set up a defensive perimeter. Smith, your E Company will bring up the rear. You cover us once we get ready to cross. Stay back, above the flatland down there. Harrington, your C Company will follow my I Company. You have your orders. Prepare to move out."

F and L Companies had moved to the left and back up the coulee, a short distance from Keogh's command. The troopers of the two companies had dismounted and stood next to their horses, guidons fluttering in the breeze. The general, with Boyer and some of the headquarters unit, moved out, further to the northeast. Kellogg spurred his mule to follow them.

Keogh raised his right arm and barked his command. "I Company, C Company, E Company, move out!"

They set their sights toward the river. Comanche was anxious, difficult to hold back from breaking into a full gallop. Riding behind Keogh was his orderly, Korn, Trumpeter Patton and I Company guidon carrier, O'Bryan. Keogh turned and looked for the dog, Joe. The last thing they needed was for the dog to bark and give away their position. But Joe was nowhere to be found.

All these years. This is it. This is the chance you need.

Three hundred yards from the river, Keogh ordered the three companies to a halt above an area of flatland. To the left, a large, dead cottonwood tree appeared. It stood alone, a ghostly white sentinel.

The ground near the river was burnt brown with clumps of sagebrush everywhere. At the river's edge, there appeared to be some light brush. He could see groves of trees and Indian tipis across the river. He scanned the river for movement.

It's too quiet, don't feel right. Where are the warriors?

Suddenly, spying through his field glasses, Keogh saw movement! His heart raced and he caught sight of the Indian women and children running to the river. Ahead of them, some young boys ran horses.

Go now!

He couldn't wait; he had to cross the river and start the attack.

Twenty-One

"Tom, you and Yates take a look at the river," said the general. The two captains had dismounted and looked through their field glasses. "From the dust to the northwest, looks like the village is still on the run."

Cooke was close. The lieutenant aimed his field glasses in the direction of the river. "I don't like it. There have to be some warriors around, protecting the women and children," he said. "It's too damn quiet. Just listen."

"Let's move to the next ridge over," the general said. "We can get a better look."

General Custer signaled for the rest of the headquarters unit, with Companies F and L, to move out of the coulee and to the ridge. A lone rider, coming from the south, headed their way.

"General! Tom!" hollered Boston Custer.

"You stupid fool," said Tom. "You're lucky as hell you didn't run into any warriors."

"I just had to catch up. Benteen is coming on," Boston told. "I passed the trumpeter."

~

"Sturgis, Bustard," Keogh shouted. Lieutenant Sturgis and Sergeant Bustard urged their horses to the head of the column. "Bustard, take Korn, Patton and a squad from your platoon to recon the river. Cover the lieutenant as he finds a crossing. If we can cross, have Patton blow the charge and then take any prisoners possible. If you see warriors, get your asses back here on the double."

Keogh turned in the saddle at the noise behind him. Above the flatland, E Company was being fired upon by a few warriors on horseback.

187

~

The handful of warriors ran toward the river and stopped at its edge. Their faces were painted red, yellow, white and black, their hair braided with red stroud cloth. Some wore loose feathered bonnets made of eagle, crow, raven, turkey and magpie feathers, others wore distinct round bonnets without a tail, made of crow feathers. A few even had short-cut style headdresses with raven, crow and hawk feathers, displaying a single row of eagle feathers down the crown. Most carried decorated rawhide shields.

Some of the warriors had long pieces of dressed buffalo-hide looped over the right shoulder and under the left arm, the assorted colors and ornamented feathers trailing down their left sides. At the other end was a short--- braided string, to which was tied a painted, sharp wooden pin. The warriors drove the wooden pins into the ground.

They were not going to retreat. They were not going to let the Seventh Cavalry ride into their village unopposed. Behind them, more warriors took up positions at the river.

~

The general and his command had now taken up positions on the ridge. L Company continued west, further down the coulee to another ridge. From there, they could support Keogh's command, if needed.

General Custer lowered his field glasses. He looked at Boston, then to the south. He walked up the ridge a short distance and heard the gunfire coming from the coulee.

"Keogh's found some women and children," said Cooke.

"He's got some warriors on him, too," Yates said. The captain looked at the general.

"Keogh has enough men. He can handle them," said the general. "Prepare to mount up. We're going in right behind them."

~

The squad from I Company pulled out of the column. With Lieutenant Sturgis in the lead, the troopers galloped for the river. Ahead of them, the Indian women and their children.

All in the three companies following Keogh could hear the Indian women screaming as they tried to reach the river. Keogh halted his command. E Company had pulled back to drive off the warriors on horseback.

Keogh watched the troopers as they stopped at the banks above the river. Slowly, their horses moved down the embankment and disappeared out of sight.

Twenty-Two

Gunfire erupted on the two companies with the general. Arrows flew through the air at the cavalrymen. The attack had come from the ridges to the east.

"Indians to the rear!" came the shout.

"Goddamn, look! Warriors behind us!" hollered a trooper.

Sporadic gunfire and more arrows rained down on the troopers, causing their horses to rear and stumble.

"Steady in the ranks!" hollered F Company First Sergeant Michael Kenney.

"Monroe! Holy Christ!" shouted Private Francis Sicfous, F Company. The private moved his horse closer and tried to grab Monroe as the trooper slid from his horse. A bullet had found the mark.

More gunfire erupted, this time from the southeast. Horses bucked and cantered sideways. Many troopers had to dismount just to control their horses. Those still in the saddle turned to see mounted Indian warriors moving along the ridges above the command. Other warriors were on foot and had taken positions on a hill.

Action was needed.

~

Lieutenant Jack Sturgis and the squad from I Company had just descended the banks of the river when a barrage of gunfire fell upon them. Sergeant Bustard and a trooper were shot off their horses while the rest of the squad tried to pull their horses up as Indian warriors picketed on the other side unleashed arrows with deadly accuracy. Warriors screamed and blew eagle-bone whistles as they raced on foot across the river.

Sturgis had only been out of sight a few minutes when Keogh heard gunfire from the river. He watched as some of the squad raced back toward his command, minus a few troopers. Close behind was Patton, followed by Korn and a horse with no rider. Korn's horse was wounded and becoming unmanageable, veering away and carrying him to the bluffs.

Jesus Christ, where's Sturgis and Bustard?

"McGucker, sound recall!" ordered Keogh. His instincts pulsed throughout his body. His blood was up.

You know what to do.

The trumpeter let out a blast from his bugle.

"Command, move out!" he ordered.

From the river, gunfire echoed. More warriors had arrived. They moved up the banks of the river, some on foot, others on ponies. Keogh glanced to his right to see the general and his command on the move as well.

With Keogh in the lead, I and C Companies galloped for fifty yards following the river, staying on the flatland. Within the terrain lay hidden, dangerous gullies that were hard to maneuver. As the troopers moved across the broken ground, many had to jump their horses over obstacles. Some of the Indian women and children who had not made the river before the cavalrymen attacked took refuge and lay unseen inside the very gullies the horses leaped over.

A few warriors appeared to the left of Keogh's command, accompanied by Indian women waving buffalo robes, hollering, and anything else to frighten the company's horses. Bullets arced from across the river, warriors poured across on foot and on horseback.

He had to do something and fast. His troopers returned fire from atop their horses, but it did little to stem the tide of surging warriors. In a matter of yards, the very ground the command traversed would drop off considerably, and they would be in close range of the warriors.

Ahead, a steep hill awaited overlooking the flatland. The hill forced Keogh to swing the command hard to the right, up a wide coulee. The companies moved in the direction of the general and his command now.

As he pulled Comanche to a stop, Keogh looked back to the river. A ghastly sight met his eyes. C Company followed I Company up the coulee as more gunfire erupted. Behind them, more warriors had crossed the river. He watched, helpless, as Sturgis rode, closely pursued. The lieutenant was knocked from his saddle by enemy fire. As the rest of C Company retreated, one C Company trooper wheeled around to try to rescue the lieutenant. He fired his revolver at the pursuing warriors even as he tried to get Sturgis mounted on his horse. The weapon clicked to empty, and the pursuers closed in for the kill.

The trooper fell to the ground in a crumpled heap after being shot several times. Sturgis lay dead. The horse broke away and took off before the warriors could capture it.

"Goddamn, you savages!" shouted Keogh firing into their midst.

With his revolver emptied, he holstered it and grabbed another. He urged Comanche up the coulee.

E Company fired toward the river, forcing the warriors to pull back. The gray horse troop moved out behind the other two companies and covered their withdraw from the river.

Once out of range, Keogh raised his field glasses and looked to the south. He hoped to catch a glimpse of the trumpeter, the last messenger the general had sent back before the companies went to the river.

There, in the distance, almost out of sight and atop the coulee, sat the trumpeter on his gray horse. He watched the action by a lone tree. Then, in the blink of an eye, they were gone.

He had to have seen what happened. He will bring Benteen.

~

General Custer and his command moved to counter the threat from behind. Warriors hidden in the tall grass opened fire, cutting down a trooper from F Company, and his horse with the first shots.

"Yates, dismount and put some fire into those warriors," ordered General Custer. The general dismounted and threw his reins to Voss. He dropped onto the ground, crawled through the sagebrush and raised his field glasses for a better look at where the warriors were coming from.

"Hold on. Wait for me to cover you!" shouted Tom. He yanked his rifle from the scabbard on his horse and dismounted, entrusting his horse to Sergeant Vickory. Tom hit the ground and crawled after the general.

"First platoon, skirmish line intervals on the double," ordered Yates.

F Company's first platoon dismounted. Every fourth trooper held his and three other troopers' horses. Sergeant Nursey led twelve men up the gradual slope of the ridge.

A small group of mounted warriors swung away from the others and moved to the northeast of the general's command. Again, some in the headquarters unit struggled to keep their horses from bolting amid the gunfire.

"If you can't hold them, get the hell off!" shouted Tom.

Kellogg's mule jumped, then kicked when it landed. He knew there was no way he could stay on it and leapt from the saddle. Now, he desperately grabbed the reins and tried to hold the animal before it ran away.

"First platoon, fire!" Yates shouted. The volley reverberated through the coulee.

"Hang on to your horse, doctor!" hollered Voss.

Doctor George Lord struggled to stay in the saddle as his

horse lunged. The horse now bucked, with the doctor barely able to hang on.

Sergeant Hughes moved his horse forward. "Hold on, doctor, I'm coming!" he shouted. The sergeant reached over and grabbed the doctor's horse by the bridle. "Easy, you, easy!"

~

Major Reno had moved his command off the skirmish line, where they were in the open and exposed, to a more protected and defensible position. The three companies were now in the timber by the river. Warriors had appeared in overwhelming numbers and the troopers burned through ammunition. The situation started to unravel after only twenty minutes. With his command spread out, communication among the three companies became impossible. Suddenly, as he stood next to Bloody Knife, a bullet slammed into the scout's head, sending pieces of flesh and brain across Reno's face. The major lost his nerve.

Reno ordered his command to their horses. Not all the companies got the message in the deafening roar of the gunfire. The major gathered the troopers who had found their horses, then led them out of the timber on a full gallop for the river. Several troopers were left in the timber and some left after the initial movement, having received no order at all.

The cavalrymen's bolt from the timber caught the warriors off guard, but Reno had neglected to throw out a skirmish line to cover the movement. The cavalrymen had no protection, and the warriors took every advantage in pursuit.

As the troopers raced for their lives, warriors rode in among them with little resistance. Men were shot from their saddles at close range, horses collapsed, throwing their riders. Others were pulled from their steeds as the warriors tried to touch them with their bare hands, to count coup. Once at the river, the troopers urged their horses to jump in wherever they could. But only a few places existed on the steep embankment to climb out once they crossed. Next came the climb up the bluffs, some three hundred feet to the top.

It was as a poorly executed plan.

Twenty-Three

Through the coulee, Keogh's command pulled their horses. Ahead of them, on the ridges above, he could see General Custer's command. To him, it appeared the general had put out some troopers in a skirmish line.

Why has Custer dismounted troops?

He pulled Comanche as quick as he could to where Porter and Lieutenant Smith stood. "What's got you two stopped?"

"There are warriors all around the general. Yates has dismounted a platoon," explained Porter.

Another round of gunfire erupted from the river, aimed squarely on Keogh's command. Troopers hollered and horses danced.

"Hold on to your damn horses," ordered C Company Sergeant Jeremiah Finley.

"Porter, take the company up the coulee a ways until we get orders," said Keogh. "McGucker!" The trumpeter pulled his horse to where they stood. Keogh never lowered his field glasses. "Get back to Harrington. Tell him to follow Porter. Get the horses between the companies. Smith, hold them here."

"Will do, Keogh," Smith answered.

C Company pulled their horses by Keogh and up the coulee. Many of the horses had become excited and hard to hold. Troopers cursed and yanked on the reins, as the animals pulled them in all directions. The company's sergeants moved in and out of the ranks, hitting the unruly horses on their backsides.

"Move those horses, now goddammit!" ordered C Company First Sergeant Bobo.

"Easy men, easy!" hollered Sergeant Finckle. "Holds on to them horses, no matter what."

Keogh was in no man's land and unsure of his next move.

Sweat ran out from beneath his hat, soaking his neckerchief and shirt collar. He didn't know what the general was doing. His chance to prove himself at the river had gone awry. Sturgis was dead and Bustard was missing, as were others from his command. As he scanned the terrain, more warriors appeared and E Company let go another volley toward the river.

Several small groups of warriors began to split up, encircling the cavalrymen, while others who had picketed themselves ran after Keogh's command. Arrows rained from gullies and ravines, then the figures dropped to disappear behind sage brush and in the tall grass.

~

General Custer had to counter the threat from the warriors who moved to the northeast. He and Tom remounted and moved for another ridge as the F Company skirmish line fired again. The headquarters unit followed.

Mounted warriors moved away from the ridge as the general and headquarters advanced. Some warriors circled to the right, hollered and shot from a safe distance. At times, one or two war-riors rode as close as they dared at the cavalrymen before pulling back.

Out of nowhere, the general spotted another group of Indian warriors appearing from the north, stationed on a nearby ridge. More were revealed to the command's front, the east, and joined the first group already firing on the general. Several warriors had dismounted unseen and now crawled through the tall grass.

"Jesus Christ!" Cooke shouted. "Where in the hell are they coming from?"

"This is one damn big village!" hollered Boyer. The scout grasped his reins tightly. With his right hand, he held his revolver. His eyes darted from the warriors and over the terrain. "There's warriors all over. We need to move!"

The warrior's fire on F Company had slackened. Those warriors on foot ran for their horses. In a flash, some of the warriors moved away and headed for the others engaging the general's command.

"Liemann to horses," ordered Yates.

F Company Trumpeter Werner Liemann blew the command. The horse holders of F Company brought the animals to those on the skirmish line.

"Company, move out!" Yates shouted.

F Company moved after the general and headquarters. There was no time to bring along their dead.

~

Tom Custer aimed his rifle at the ridge to the northeast. He closed his left eye, took a deep breath and squeezed the trigger ever so slightly. "That will keep you asses back!" he hollered. "Let's get after them."

"Easy Tom," warned the general as he raised his field glasses.

"You need to move on them now, Custer!" yelled Boyer. "More warriors will be coming."

The enemy was everywhere. They ran from one spot to another before a trooper could fire a shot. They shot arrows high into the sky, then disappeared into the terrain and slithered closer to the cavalrymen.

F Company had reunited with the general's command, but they were in the open, easy targets with no cover on the ridge. It was time to move.

"We have got to get off of this ridge and onto better fighting ground," said General Custer.

"What are you thinking?" Tom asked.

"First, we're going to drive these warriors off for good," said

199

the general. "Boyer, are there any places to cross further down the river?"

"Might be some to the northwest," replied Boyer. "I can't be sure. Been so long since I was through there."

"Cooke, get a message to Keogh," ordered the general. "Tell him to move across the coulee and cover our flank. Have him take that ridge to the north. Tell him to wait for word from us and to keep the way open for Benteen and the pack train."

~

Down the coulee and through the gunpowder smoke, a horse and rider came. Keogh strained to see who it might be.

Sharrow? Jesus Christ!

Time stood still for Myles Keogh, and the moment was not lost on him. He looked south for Benteen and McDougall, but saw only Indian warriors dotting the landscape.

Most were on foot. Those on horses kept well back, out of the cavalrymen's firing range for now. Most of the warriors carried bows and arrows, but some did have firearms. Some even carried repeating rifles.

The warriors were now between Keoghs' and Benteen's command. He could feel his hands shake.

Stay calm and keep your head about you. Keep everybody together!

Sharrow pulled his horse up and dismounted. "Captain, the general is moving out to drive off the warriors," he said. "You're to follow and cover the river. Set up on the ridge to the north there, find a good defensive position and wait for Benteen and the pack train."

"Understood Sharrow," said Keogh. "Patton, get word to Harrington to follow us across this coulee. Tell Smith to cover us and the general. Then tell him to come on once we make the ridge. Sharrow, you had better stay with us."

"I'm the sergeant major of this outfit," Sharrow proudly said. "I got to hurry and get back, captain. The general will be on the move."

Keogh watched the sergeant major move back up the coulee. Just before he lost sight of the sergeant in the smoke and terrain, he caught a glimpse of the general's command. They were forming to charge!

He's moving on them---he knows what he's doing.

"Trumpeter, to horses. Let's move out," he ordered.

McGucker let out a blast from his bugle, telling all those in Keogh's command to mount and follow.

~

Benteen considered the message. *Benteen come on. Big Village. Be quick. Bring Pack.*

W. W. Cooke & bring packs. He handed it to Captain Weir.

"Where is General Custer?" Benteen asked the trumpeter.

"About three miles from here," Martini answered.

"Is he being attacked?"

"Yes," said Martini.

"Your horse has been wounded," Benteen pointed out.

The young trumpeter looked at his gray horse. A smile accompanied a nervous laugh.

"Join your troop," Benteen ordered. "Companies, forward."

They moved ahead, with Weir and his orderly a short distance behind them. Around a bend, the valley of the Little Bighorn River came in sight. Gunfire cracked.

Benteen and Weir watched the action unfold to their front. Several hundred yards away, down the valley and next to the river, a fight played out, but the scene didn't make sense. Both captains could plainly see Indian warriors riding around and attacking cavalrymen. Some of the troopers looked to be in a makeshift skirmish line, while others rode their horses across the river. Lieutenant Godfrey of K Company joined them. Before anyone spoke, the troopers in their command informed them that mounted Indians were coming their way.

"Those are scouts," said Weir.

The Indians pulled up one hundred yards away, and the three officers galloped to them. They were the Crow scouts, Hairy Moccasin, White Man Runs Him and Goes Ahead. They and another Crow by the name of Curly had ridden with Boyer and General Custer's command. Curly had left the others some distance back.

White Man Runs Him tried to communicate with the officers in English, but his was too broken for them to make sense of it. Godfrey started using sign language and the Crow responded. A flurry of exchanges continued, then stopped abruptly when the Crow looked back on the trail he and his companions had come from.

"What did he say, Godfrey?" Benteen asked.

The lieutenant hesitated. He looked to the river, then back at Benteen. "Big village with lots of Sioux. He says Boyer told them to go on back."

"What about Custer?" asked Weir.

"Made it seem like Custer was going to cross and attack but couldn't. He says Custer is in a fight!"

The Crow joined the three companies as Benteen led his command up the bluffs.

Twenty-Four

General Custer, the headquarters unit and companies F and L began to move in a northeastern direction, a company on each side, riding in columns of twos. With their revolvers pulled, the trooper's horses loped into a trot. The Indians to their front scattered, their ponies, lean and fast, keeping well ahead of the bigger Army horses. Some warriors stopped and picked up their fellow warriors who had been hiding and firing from positions in the tall grass.

Keogh led the two companies out of the coulee and up the hill. The terrain was not overly rugged, but he'd ordered his troopers to dismount for the gradual climb. To his command's left, an expansive grass ridge ran next to the river. To the right, the general and his command.

From the south, warriors filled the landscape and followed Keogh's command. The gray horse troop moved to stop their advance.

~

Lieutenant Algernon Smith led his E Company up the gradual slope and out of the coulee. The ridges and hills the gray horse troop moved over were deceiving. One minute, a mounted trooper could see for a good distance, then in the blink of an eye, the terrain would drop, leaving one feeling disoriented and defenseless against an attack.

A few shots kicked up the ground as the company made a ridge. When Smith saw the warriors showing no fear of the advancing cavalrymen, he knew what to do. "Hohmeyer!" he shouted to his first sergeant. "Dismount first platoon. Skirmish line."

E Company First Sergeant Frederick Hohmeyer swung his charcoal gray horse around and ordered the trumpeter to deliver the command. "E Company, first platoon, halt. Dismount. Skirmish line intervals. Advance on foot," he ordered.

The men of E Company's first platoon dismounted and ran a few yards ahead. Each trooper held his own horse, as the situation warranted quick action. On the far right, Corporal George Brown was the end of the skirmish line. Now, Brown had no one but his horse, a big gray by the name of Julian, behind him. To his right, a lonely hillside. From the corner of his eye, Brown caught a glimpse of the advancing warriors.

Corporal Brown's heart raced and the sweat from his forehead poured over his eyes. He squeezed the trigger on his Springfield rifle and placed a fairly accurate shot between the warriors. But they continued forward, then dropped, hidden from view. "Shit! Where the hell are they?" Brown's horse pulled back on him, the sudden jerk causing him to lose his balance for a moment. He yanked on the reins. "Dammit, Julian. Stop, you son of a bitch!"

One arrow, then a second, a third, now a fourth, flew in his direction, the entire E Company line taking fire. Brown fired into the clump of grass and sagebrush ahead of them.

George Brown wanted to run, but his legs refused. A fear like no other he had ever experienced gripped him. Amid the noise, everything went silent as he lost his grip on the bullet he'd retrieved from the leather belt around his waist. The corporal pulled his Colt revolver, cocked the hammer and fired.

No more arrows came his way.

~

"Command halt!" Benteen called out.

On the bluffs above the river, what was left of Major Reno's shattered command was found. Men lay wounded while others scrambled up the steep bluffs. Horses were being gathered and held by a few troopers. No organized resistance was in place. For now, the warriors stayed at the river, busy with looting the dead.

Reno grabbed the reins to his horse and rode to meet Benteen. "For God's sake, Benteen, halt your command and help me. I've lost half my men and could do no better than I have done."

"Where is Custer?" asked Benteen.

"I've had no communication from the general since my orders in the valley," he told.

Gunfire from a group of warriors on a hill to the north kicked up the ground around Reno's survivors. More and more warriors were gathering.

"I'll take my company and drive off those warriors," said Weir. "D Company, advance." D Company followed their captain at a gallop.

Reno looked to the river. The major then unloaded his revolver at no presentable target.

Benteen eyed Godfrey. "Take your company and cover Weir's flank. Secure the bluffs above the river and cover any troops still coming up," he ordered.

"Will do, captain," Godfrey said.

Lieutenant Godfrey and his company pulled out and galloped ahead. Benteen and Reno followed.

More troopers were arriving, Lieutenant Hare among them. The lieutenant was shaken and excited as he dismounted and ran to Benteen. "We just got whipped like hell! I don't know how many men we lost, but son of a bitch, they're dead!"

~

"D Company, first platoon, dismount!" shouted Weir. "First platoon, advance on foot."

The troopers of D Company advanced up the gradual slope of the hill under scattered fire from the warriors. No casualties had occurred yet. Many warriors had raced off. They seemed more occupied with some type of situation to the north. Two sets of volleys drove away the few who had stayed.

When the troopers of D Company crested the hill, they had a commanding view. Behind them, to the south, Captain Benteen was organizing their fellow troopers. Some from Reno's command still straggled up the bluffs. When they turned their attention back to the north, they could see blue clad troopers on gray horses as they rode over the ridges, some two miles away. It had to be General Custer's command.

Twenty-Five

The two companies Keogh led had gotten out of the coulee and made the ridge. Up ahead, to the northeast, the general and all accompanying him headed for a prominent hill overlooking the area. To the south, Keogh scanned the terrain in hopes of seeing Benteen and McDougall. He saw neither.

What he did see filled him with despair.

Groups of warriors filled the landscape and fired on E Company. Most were shirtless and blended into the terrain and buffalo grass. Many had painted themselves. Some wore their hair in braids and were dressed only in a breechclout and leggings. A few warriors wore the big feathered headdress with the long tail to it. Some of the warriors carried shields, with animals and other symbols painted on them.

To the southwest, more warriors had gathered. They'd left their ponies well back near the bluffs, then crawled in the tall grass toward Keogh's ridge.

"First platoon, dismounted skirmish line, Varden," ordered Keogh. "Cover Smith."

Sergeant Varden led the platoon on foot out onto the ridge facing southeast, above the coulee. The troopers of I Company's first platoon dispersed at intervals and knelt to fire.

"Get me Harrington," ordered Keogh to the trumpeter.

~

Keogh and Comanche waited as C Company pulled their horses past I Company. Lieutenant Henry Harrington and trumpeter McGucker came Keogh's way. The lieutenant was covered in dust. His wide brimmed hat, which had once been white, was now gray from dirt and sweat. His blue shirt stuck to his chest, soaked.

207

"You made it," said Keogh. "Your company in order?"

"Yes, captain. We are ready when you need us," Harrington said.

"Good, we're moving out. Your company will be the advance," Keogh said. "Move for that hill. Send out flankers as you advance. Looks like the general is heading there. Keep your eyes on your backside, to the southwest, above the river."

"Consider it done, captain," Harrington responded. The lieutenant pulled his horse away and back to his company.

Lieutenant Smith and his E Company now galloped onto the ridge and past I Company. Smith saw Keogh, dismounted and pulled his horse his way.

"Good work, Smith," Keogh said.

"Warriors are streaming up the coulee, Keogh," Smith informed. "Hundreds, maybe more!"

"Rest your company here for a bit. We're moving shortly for the hill."

~

The warriors following Smith's E Company pulled back to stay out of firing range. One warrior kept on, defiantly waving his Winchester rifle back and forth over his head. He turned and faced the mass of warriors following him to show he was not afraid. Dressed only in a breechclout and moccasins, he carried a war club and knife in a beaded scabbard at his waist. His body was painted with white dots, a few symbols stroked across his face. A single feather adorned his hair, with an eagle bone whistle wrapped loosely around his neck.

Bullets from I Company kicked up the ground all around the warrior's horse. The horse was a paint, with a broad chest and strong hindquarters. Both the warrior and the horse showed no fear. He turned and shouted at the troopers of the Seventh Cavalry, then pulled his horse to the left and disappeared with his warriors in the broken terrain.

Twenty-Six
The Hill

Keogh breathed a sigh of relief. The three companies he commanded were now on the verge of reuniting. He pulled Comanche up the hill where his troopers stood ready to deploy.

You're lucky as hell to find such a place. Get them set up.

If they could set up good defensive positions, the hill would give his command control of the nearby terrain and allow them to wait for Benteen and the pack train.

C Company First Sergeant Bobo galloped from the hill. "Captain, Lieutenant Harrington sends word. There are no signs of warriors behind the hill. It slopes into a swale and there is a good ravine to shelter the horses. General Custer is there waiting. Calhoun has dismounted and is getting his skirmish line in order to cover you."

The troopers of E and I companies pulled their horses up onto the hill where part of C Company sat. The heat and recent action had taken a toll on the animals. Warriors still followed from the south and a significant number gathered to the east. Both groups stayed just out of the cavalrymen's firing range. Some of the warriors lay prone on the ground and sniped at the companies with rifle fire, as small groups splintered off from the others and crawled closer to the hill. Now, arrows started to drop on the command from the ravines and hills to the southwest.

Troopers hollered and shouted, their horses cantered sideways and jerked against their reins.

"Hold your damn horses!" shouted Lieutenant Smith. "You lose those horses, you'll be in a world of shit!"

The platoon from Keogh's I Company was still in skirmish line order under the leadership of Varden, protecting the rear of the command. A squad from C Company's first platoon, led by Sergeant Finley, was deployed along the ridge covering Varden's flank.

Lieutenant James Calhoun organized his L Company skirmish line and then walked it down the hill some distance. Sergeant Cashan anchored the left, with Sergeant Warren on the right. Lieutenant Crittenden stood behind Warren, and First Sergeant James Butler posted behind Cashan. The L Company horses were pulled down the slope of the hill for the ravine to conceal them.

Officers' call carried over the sound of gunfire.

"Patton, sound recall for the C Company squad and Varden," ordered Keogh. He and Calhoun made their way up the hill to the group now huddled around the general.

~

General George Custer scanned the Little Bighorn River. He lowered his field glasses as Mitch Boyer and Lieutenant Riley pulled their horses' up and dismounted.

"Report lieutenant," said the general.

"Sir, we followed the warriors around the hill at the end of this hogback ridge, to our front, here," Riley said. He pointed at the ridge Keogh and the rest stood on. "Once on the other side of that hill, the valley opens and there are some ridges to follow to the river. We took some light fire, but it was hard to get a fix on where it came from. The warriors seemed hell bent on getting to the river."

"Did you see any women and children?" General Custer asked.

"Yes, sir. By the river," replied Riley. "They're everywhere, sir. There has to be thousands of them!"

"Can we cross down there, Boyer?" the general asked.

"Can't be sure. Even if we find a crossing, there are too many for us to handle alone."

"We don't need all of them," General Custer said. "It's time to make our play. I'm taking headquarters, along with E and F Companies, to find a crossing. I will send a messenger back for you,

Keogh. You hold the back door open for Benteen. By the time the pack train gets here, we will have secured a crossing."

"Understood, general," Keogh said. "We will hold here."

"Prepare to move out," ordered the general. "Riley, you and your squad lead out."

The general, Boyer, Kellogg and some of the others moved away until it was only Keogh, Tom, Cooke and Calhoun who remained together. The four looked towards the river. Fleeing figures spurred dust clouds. The roar of gunfire had increased.

Tom smiled, then reached his hand out to Keogh. "When Benteen gets here, ask him what in the hell took him so long."

"You can ask him yourself when this is all over," he replied.

Cooke looked at Keogh. "So long, Keogh. You know, heading back east don't sound too bad right about now."

Tom and Cooke mounted their horses. "Keep them off us so we can get across," said Tom. "Watch out for Jimmi there, Keogh. If something happens to him, I'll never hear the end of it." He pulled his horse away.

"I'll make sure we get word to you when we find a place to cross," Cooke promised.

"Good luck," said Keogh.

Cooke rode to catch up with the general's command and Calhoun moved for his company. For a moment, Keogh had time to himself. He thought of Nelly, how desperately he wanted off this hill and to be by her side. His heart ached for her and all he could think of was how foolish he had been all these years. She would be waiting for him. He was determined to survive.

You will make it back to her! You are not going to die here! Fight them like they've never been fought before, Keogh. Remember what Comstock always said, take the fight to an Indian!

His heart started to beat faster and his hands began to sweat. An uneasy feeling--- one that made him want to run away--- washed over him with fury and intensity, like none he had ever experienced before. It always seemed to come when death was close---but never this powerful!

Snap out of it….control your fears.

He surveyed the scene before him.

Below the hill, Calhoun's L Company stood their ground, holding back the warriors from the south and east with their controlled and accurate fire. When Keogh turned his field glasses to the southwest, he was mortified at how quickly the Indians had continued with their advance above the river. They fanned out, moving to the northwest. From here, the warriors had now taken a ridge that threatened his command's right flank.

What worried him was the pack train. They should be getting close, close enough to hear the gunfire, he reasoned. They would have a rough time getting through the warriors. The hills were covered with them. The sick feeling again found his stomach. He saw no one.

Benteen, come on. We need you!

~

Thirty minutes after joining Reno's command, Benteen sent Lieutenant Hare for the pack train that was still coming on. He was to cut out two mules with ammunition and bring them back to the bluffs.

Major Reno had left the hill with a detail of troopers to look for Lieutenant Hodgson. When last seen, the lieutenant had been wounded on the flight across the river. A trooper had stopped to help Hodgson who had lost his horse. The trooper tried to pull the lieutenant out of the river and to the other side, when a bullet hit Hodgson and the trooper lost his hold on the lieutenant.

The major had found the lieutenant's body close to the river but was unable to bury him due to the many warriors still in the area. The major took what personal items he could and led the detail that accompanied him back for the bluffs.

At the same time Reno's party returned, other troopers appeared from hiding out in the timber. They had not gotten the order to pull out and had stayed.

Weir returned from his successful advance on the warriors and dismounted, heading for a group of officers assembled around Benteen. Hare had arrived with the ammunition. Captain McDougall and Lieutenant Mathey with the pack train, had pulled in as well. Moylan and French were there, with lieutenants Varnum, Wallace and Godfrey. Reno joined them.

"I have Custer's trail," said Weir. "It goes behind the ridge my company is on. We can hear gunfire, plain as day. It has to be Custer. Keogh's orderly, Korn, made it back. Said his horse was wounded at the river as they looked for a crossing."

"We're surrounded by Indians and we ought to remain here," advised Reno.

"Custer can take care of himself," said Benteen.

Silence fell among the officers. Gunfire, although faint, peppered through the still air.

"I think we ought to be down there with Custer," McDougall said.

"Well, I'm going to Custer, even if the rest of you will not!" snapped Weir.

"You cannot go. You and your company will be killed if you try," Reno said.

Captain Weir remounted his horse and rode to where his D Company was stationed. Lieutenant Edgerly and Sergeant Flanagan of D Company watched him ride by.

"Troop mount!" shouted Edgerly.

D Company settled onto their horses and took off after their captain. They were a little over three miles from Keogh's command now.

Keogh pulled Comanche to the right and down the slope of the hill. They moved for his I Company. Porter had taken the company to the backside of the hill and deployed in reserve, ready to support C and L Companies if needed.

"Porter, take the horses to the ravine back there, by C and L Company's horses. It's the best place to protect them. You take second platoon and fan out on this hogback ridge to the west. The Indians are coming up from the river. Don't let them outflank us. We can't let them get between us and the general. Patton, on me," Keogh ordered.

He and the trumpeter urged their horses back up the hill. They moved for the ground where C Company was deployed. Harrington left where part of his C Company was stationed and pulled his horse to where Keogh stood.

"Good work securing the hill and finding a place to protect the horses," said Keogh.

"Thank you, captain," replied Harrington.

"Keep your company firing toward the southwest. Support Calhoun and cover his right flank," he ordered.

"Yes, sir," Harrington said.

~

After receiving his orders, Porter led I Company into the fight, making sure the company horse holders were concealed in the ravine below the hill. He then moved his way up the hill, leading I Company's second platoon into position on the hogback ridge. The lieutenant placed the troopers in skirmish line order, at intervals along the ridge. Between them and closer to the hill where Keogh and Comanche waited, Sergeant Varden deployed I Company's first platoon. Their position ran into the right flank of C Company.

From atop the hill, Keogh watched the deployment of his company, proud of his men as they fanned out and faced the advancing Indians. I Company began to fire. Puffs of smoke rose above the troopers.

God, how thin and spread out we are.

Amid the smoke and roar of gunfire, Keogh tried to concentrate. He was relieved the company's horses were sheltered and the companies deployed. He knew more action would soon be needed. He looked to the northwest, through his field glasses. Nothing had been seen of the general's command since the two companies had turned down the ridge toward the river, in hopes of capturing the non-combatants.

No one and nothing.

Twenty-Seven
To the River

General Custer had the fleeing village before him. He halted his command below the hill at the end of the hogback ridge. It was time for action. Across the river, he and his command could see thousands of people and horses moving about. It was a scene of panic and confusion.

"Yates!" called the general.

Captain George Yates let his horse break into a trot for the headquarters unit. "Yes, general."

"Captain, take your company and go with Boyer. Find a crossing," ordered the general. "I will take headquarters and E Company further down to look for one as well."

"What about covering us? There has to be some warriors close," asked Yates. "Besides, look at all these people. My God, Custer, look at all of them. Don't go splitting us up!"

"You have your orders, captain. Send a messenger if you are able to cross," said the general. "If you get a chance to capture some women and children, take them."

Yates looked down the slope of the hill, in the direction of the river and the non-combatants. He turned in his saddle, glancing toward the general, then past the two companies and the ridge they had just ridden over.

"We are close, captain," the general said. "Stay with me a little longer and we will get through it."

General Custer pulled away, headquarters and E Company following him to the north. After going a short distance, they turned to the west and traveled along a ridge which gradually took the command to the river. Next to the ridge, a ravine sat. It was filled with some timber and brush. The mouth to the ravine opened just above the river's bank.

To the general's left, he could see Boyer, Yates and F Company on some flatland near the river, scouting for a crossing. Now, arrows whistled through the air, launched by a hidden and unseen enemy and from seemingly all directions. The arrows landed all around the companies, making troopers and horses edgy.

General Custer, Tom, Voss and Sharrow galloped to the river's edge. Around the river's bend they could see the non-combatants and they could see the cavalrymen.

"Bank's too steep," said the general. "We must find another crossing."

"We need to hurry," Tom said. "Look to the northwest."

Mounted warriors galloped out of the immense pony herd. They raced in circles and back and forth, readying the ponies for a fight.

Light gunfire came at the companies from across the river. Tom and Sharrow returned fire.

"Smith!" shouted the general.

Lieutenant Algernon Smith nudged his charcoal gray horse forward.

"Take your company over to the west and see if we can cross. Keep your eyes open for warriors," he ordered. "If we can cross, send back word. We're holding here to link up with Yates."

"Understood, general," replied Smith. The lieutenant turned his horse back to the command. "E Company, forward."

The gray horse troop moved around the river's banks, to the west, and for another part of the river. Scattered shots kicked up the ground all around them, yet they continued on.

"Voss, get to Yates. Find out if he can cross, then get back here to us," the general ordered.

"Yes, general," said Voss.

The chief trumpeter pulled his horse to the left and moved for F Company. He had not gone far when an Indian rode up out of the riverbank. Voss pulled his gray horse up, startled at the sight of the blue leggings and red-painted upper body and face. In his left hand, the warrior carried a huge lance shaped like a bow.

As quick as the Indian appeared, he pulled his painted pony back to the river and disappeared. Voss continued on toward F Company. As he neared the river, he could see Yates had sent a squad to cross.

Gunfire rained down on the squad from across the river before they could even attempt a crossing. One horse was hit, the trooper was unhorsed and scrambled back to the company. More gunfire came from across the river. Voss and his horse had been targeted. The trumpeter and his horse both lay mortally wounded in the grass. F Company rode past them towards the headquarters unit.

"Dismount!" ordered the general.

From the north, groups of warriors had moved in, targeting the troopers with arrows before crawling even closer through gullies and the tall grass. General Custer raised his field glasses to the west and looked for the gray horse troop.

~

E Company had found the non-combatants. The people screamed, women, children and the elderly ran from the river. In a nearby ravine they gathered for shelter. Smith and his troop looked for a crossing amid the chaos.

But warriors took positions in the brush and timber along the river's edge. They were not many in number, but they were determined to protect their people.

E Company halted at the river's edge, and Smith moved ahead with a squad as others in the company set up to cover the crossing. Gunfire and arrows met them in a deadly storm. Two troopers were shot off their horses, Lieutenant Smith was wounded, only remaining on his horse thanks to his men tying his hands to the pommel of the saddle before they retreated.

221

~

With his command reunited, General Custer knew it was time to return to Keogh's position. It would take his entire force to cross together, to capture the non-combatants.

"Yates, cover us as we go back for Keogh!" shouted the general.

"Will do, general," replied Yates. "F Company, dismount."

"Tom, you make sure Smith is brought along. I'll take E Company and lead us out," hollered the general.

The general and Boyer led E Company out of the ravine and back for the hill at the end of the hogback ridge. The headquarters unit came next, with Sergeants Hughes and Vickory, Autie Reed and Boston Custer. Doctor Lord and Sharrow pulled Smith on his horse while Tom and Cooke brought up the rear. Kellogg was having trouble getting remounted on his mule. The mule circled and jumped amid the noise of the fighting.

F Company's horses had been pulled into the ravine, where the brush and trees afforded some shelter. Part of the company faced the northeast, the other to the north with the horse holders responsible for double the horses---securing eight rather than the usual four. The captain needed every extra trooper on the skirmish line to cover the general's withdraw.

From the south, a few warriors crossed the river and moved undetected toward F Company, their bodies and faces painted, some with colored stripes of red, black, yellow, green and white. They stopped a hundred yards from the ravine and crawled through the tall buffalo grass.

A group of Indian women had followed the warriors and, concealed by heavy brush and timber, began creeping up the riverbank. From there, they could see the unprotected horse holders of F Company. The Indian women waited.

Without warning, arrows and gunfire filled the air above F Company. Indian women screamed, hollered, threw stones and waved sticks. The horse holders were completely taken by surprise. Horses reared and kicked, swinging the men around in circles as they tried to hold on. F Company's horses stampeded, and with them went the trooper's extra ammunition.

In the attack, Kellogg had been shot off his mule. The animal ran to the river, carrying his notes in the saddlebags.

"F Company, second platoon!" screamed Yates as he ran to their position. "Riley, swing your platoon to the south, now!"

The Indian women had disappeared. F Company's second platoon opened fire and halted the warriors coming from the south.

"First platoon, advance on foot," Yates ordered. "Hurry men, move!"

F Company's first platoon ran up the ravine, trying to catch up to E Company.

Twenty-Eight

Looking from the hogback ridge Keogh watched warriors, on foot and on horseback, gathering.

The troopers from I Company fired, but more and more crawled toward them, unfazed. A moving Cheyenne or Sioux warrior was a hard target to hit. They popped up, fired their rifle or shot an arrow, then hit the ground and crawled closer. Using ravines and coulees as routes of infiltration, the warriors hid behind clumps of sagebrush for concealment.

A sight caught Keogh's attention and gave him hope. Horses moved in the distance---ones who appeared to be carrying riders wearing blue coats. He thought they were scouts from Gibbon and Terry's command, come from downriver. He trained his field glasses on the movement, but there was something strange about the group as they rode out of the ravine, directly toward Keogh's men.

At the head of the procession rode a warrior wearing a faded blue Army coat. He looked straight ahead, unfazed by the gunfire. Directly behind him rode two warriors, side by side, with more galloping beyond. Many of the figures wore old faded blue Army coats, cut up and decorated in all types of ways. The warrior's faces were painted in an assortment of colors. Some had their hair in a knot, tied up above their forehead, a single eagle feather through the knot. Their ponies painted in different colors, with various designs and symbols.

These were no Army scouts. These were Indian warriors coming to destroy his command!

~

Troopers hollering and shouting down the hill to the east caught Keogh's attention. Below the ridge, the hill sloped into a swale where the horses of the three companies were held in a natural ravine. There, the gunfire had irritated the mounts, making their control near impossible.

A ridge, running parallel to the ravine where the horses were being held, loomed behind Keogh's command. For now, it was free of Indian warriors. Keogh lowered his field glasses, debating if he should send a squad from his company to protect the horse holders and horses.

Back to the west he looked for the warrior in the blue coat and the others that followed him. They had disappeared.

Goddammit, think!

There wasn't a sign of the pack train or Benteen. All he saw were Indians on their bellies, firing at L Company.

Advancing to their position would be tough for Benteen's command, plus the pack train, given the horde of warriors firing at L Company. Regardless, Keogh knew if Benteen came on, the Indians would not be able to concentrate solely on his command.

Damn it, Benteen, come on!

Time was running out, and Myles Keogh knew it. Bullets whipped by, humming like a giant beehive, a sound he had not heard since the war. The air was heavy with arrows and gunpowder smoke. The noise was deafening. Something had to be done and soon.

Comanche pulled against his reins, angry, eager to do more than observe. He wanted to fight. "Easy, boy. Settle down." Comanche pulled against Keogh, stamped and snorted. "Easy, boy, come on now."

He directed the unruly horse behind C Company, to where Harrington stood. The lieutenant was in control of his company as he moved behind his troopers and shouted encouragement.

The company's gunfire had kept the Indians from further advancing from the southwest for now. The lieutenant stood behind one platoon with Sergeant Finckle. The other platoon was being commanded by First Sergeant Bobo and Sergeant Finley.

"Get me Lieutenant Calhoun, on the double," Keogh said to Patton.

This is it, Keogh. You know what to do. They're about to enclose you in a ring. Keep a corridor open for Benteen. He is coming.

Twenty-Nine

In a matter of minutes, the trumpeter returned with Calhoun.

"We can't stay on this damn hill much longer! If we do, the Indians will outflank us somewhere. There are too many warriors," said Keogh. "The general has gone to the northwest, and I'm worried about your right flank." He pointed to the southwest, where warriors were clearly seen fanning out and taking positions. "Hell, when Benteen does appear, I don't think he can get through. Something has to be done and now!"

"What do you propose?" asked Calhoun. The lieutenant put down his field glasses and wiped the sweat from his eyes. "I don't think Benteen is coming."

Keogh heard the desperation in his voice. He turned to Harrington. "Take your C Company up the ridge to the southwest. Drive them back to the river," he ordered. "Don't go too far, though. Keep your horses back behind your line."

Lieutenant Harrington said nothing in response. Keogh wasn't sure he'd heard a word. The lieutenant stared in the direction he was to take C Company, Indians were everywhere.

"Harrington," Keogh said again. "You hearing me, lieutenant?"

"Yes, sir, Captain Keogh." The lieutenant quickly saluted, never taking his eyes off the advancing warriors.

"Calhoun, swing part of your platoon on the right to cover them," Keogh said. "I will bring a squad over from my first platoon to help cover the west."

"Will do, Keogh," said Calhoun.

Keogh remounted Comanche. Before he left Calhoun, he looked the lieutenant in the eye. "Benteen is coming. Keep your men calm and firing. That's all we have to do. We just need to buy the general some time."

Calhoun stared up at him, then shook his head. "You know,

Keogh, I never thought it could come to something like this out here. I should have said more to my wife the day we left."

With a nudge from Keogh, Comanche moved closer. He extended his hand.

Calhoun stepped back and saluted Keogh. The lieutenant then turned to his company and shouted, "L Company, United States Seventh Cavalry, let them know who we are! Let them know we are here to stay! Sergeant Warren, take a squad from second platoon, cover C Company!"

~

The horse holders of C Company pulled the horses up the hill to the C company position. Keogh watched as each platoon took turns mounting their horses.

Harrington was the only C Company officer, but the company did have three strong and experienced sergeants. The situation was not ideal to send a company with so many inexperienced troopers into. Keogh knew it, but he had no other options. He hoped Harrington and the sergeants could keep the company together.

"C Company, column of fours," ordered Harrington.

It didn't matter now. Not a man riding in C Company flinched or balked. The troopers did as ordered.

The men of C Company wore white hats and riding their Roan Sorrel horses, the company had a distinctive look. C Company galloped down the hill with their rifles hanging to their right side, attached to a leather strap slung across their chest. The Seventh Cavalry's troopers carried the 1873 Springfield Carbine. It was a powerful rifle, capable of hitting a target from three hundred yards.

Initially, the Indians that were the closest to the hill began to run away and disappear into the ravines and gullies as C Company advanced. The sound of revolver fire could be heard coming from the company.

Keogh pressed his field glasses to his eyes and watched C Company move further up the ridge. They rode four abreast as they galloped onto a flat part of the ridge that would have given them command of the entire area.

"There. Stop there, Harrington," Keogh whispered.

C Company kept going. They turned west, and headed toward the river.

"Form your skirmish line, Harrington!" hollered Keogh.

C Company disappeared further into the terrain. Warriors ran in all directions. Some hid in the tall grass and gullies, then waited for the cavalrymen to pass.

"You damn fool, Harrington!" Keogh shouted. "Stop and dismount those men!"

~

"Lieutenant," Sergeant Bobo shouted. "We should dismount, sir."

Harrington never responded. He continued to take C Company further into the broken terrain.

It was hard to see C Company through all the smoke and uneven terrain. Keogh and Patton pulled their horses further away from the hill, to the southwest. Then Keogh caught a glimpse of the action. A terrible feeling of fear gripped him, and panic set in as he knew he'd made a colossal mistake. "Goddamn you, Harrington!"

Lieutenant Harrington and his C Company had driven the Indians back toward the river, but he'd taken the company too far up the ridge in doing so.

"Lieutenant, we need to dismount now!" shouted Bobo.

Harrington pulled his horse up, then wheeled the animal beside his men. "First platoon, dismount," he ordered. "Skirmish line on the double!"

Sergeant Finley and his first platoon dismounted. They walked out onto the ridge to start and anchor the far left of the skirmish line. The platoon's horses were pulled behind a small knoll. Finley held on to his own horse.

Further up the ridge, Harrington led the remainder of C Company, the terrain becoming more and more deceiving the further they advanced. Seemingly level one minute, the ground would then drop. Arrows flew at troopers from ravines and gullies. Warriors hollered and blew eagle bone whistles that made a shrill and eerie sound.

"Bobo, have Finckle take second platoon, move on up this ridge," Harrington ordered.

"Lieutenant, what about the horses?" hollered Bobo. "We should get them behind the line."

"There's no time," said Harrington. "Put some fire into those warriors!"

~

Hundreds of warriors had moved in close to the ground near C Company. Encouraged and implored on by the warrior chief in the blue Army coat, the warriors that had ran from the company initially had regrouped and now poured a tremendous amount of fire on C Company.

Keogh saw several Indian warriors to the company's front and right flank mass for an assault. Only half of C Company looked to be in a skirmish line. Some troopers on the line attempted to fire their rifles and hold their horses at the same time.

In disbelief, Keogh watched the tragedy unfold. He felt like he was in a terrible dream. Comanche pulled hard against him. Bullets hit close and kicked up dirt on the ground near them. The Indians had him and Comanche in their sights. "Move, Harrington!" In agony, Keogh looked on as Indians swarmed over the troopers of

C Company.
Get them out of there!

~

"What now, lieutenant?" hollered Bobo.

Harrington never responded. The lieutenant emptied his revolver, reloaded it, and pulled his horse hard to the north.

"Stop running men!" ordered Finckle. "Hold fast!"

An eruption of gunfire engulfed the second platoon. Sergeant August Finckle and his men were attacked by hundreds of warriors. Several troopers were shot from their horses. Those on foot had thrown down their rifles and now fired their revolvers. A few in the skirmish line tried to remount their horses, but Indians were on them in seconds.

Hand-to- hand fighting raged on the ridge. Troopers ran in all directions. Horses were scattered and running everywhere.

Keogh witnessed a mounted Indian warrior immerge out of the mass with the C Company guidon. The warrior waved the guidon and chased troopers with it, trying to count coup.

The men of second platoon were overran and destroyed.

A group of C Company troopers burst from the clouds of smoke and moved south, firing their revolvers from atop their horses. They attempted to break through the ring of warriors surrounding them.

"Go! Go!" screamed Keogh. Tears ran down his face. He put down his field glasses and wiped them with his sleeve before returning his gaze to the slaughter.

Four troopers were pursued as they rode south. Everything went silent as he watched them leave his sight. It was like their horses were flying over the broken landscape, their feet running on air.

In silent horror, Keogh witnessed the destruction of C Company. The surviving members of the company ran back in his direction. Some on foot, others on horse. He closed his eyes and heard Nelly's warning again drift back to him.

Suddenly a bullet crashed into Comanche's neck, snapping Keogh back to reality. The horse screamed in pain, threw his head up and down violently, over and over, blood running down his neck.

"Easy, boy, easy!" shouted Keogh. He tried to hold the horse, but Comanche reared up on his hind legs. When he came down, Keogh pulled himself onto the horse. "Patton, sound recall, now!" The trumpeter didn't move or respond, he just stared in the direction of where C Company was being destroyed. He was frozen, in a state of shock at what he had just witnessed. "Patton! Patton! Snap out of it boy. They are gone, sound recall for the rest. Then get back to the hill and let Calhoun know what happened. Tell him to cover us. Wait for me on the hill. Let's go boy."

Comanche galloped in the direction of the C Company troopers running down the ridge. Keogh pulled a revolver out of its holster and cocked the hammer, drawing a bead on a pursuing warrior.

His second shot dropped the warrior. C Company troopers continued running his way.

"Stop your running! Form a skirmish line!" Keogh ordered. "You on horses, turn around and help me!"

~

Further down the ridge, to the east, C Company's first platoon now attempted a stand. The remaining troops had taken up defensive positions on the little knoll. It was a heroic gesture, but futile. Sergeant Finley tried to hold his horse, Carlo, and fire his revolver, while keeping his platoon together.

"Keep firing, keep firing!" ordered Finley. "Carlo! Carlo! No! Carlo, no!"

The horse was hit by an arrow. It danced sideways and pulled the sergeant off balance.

"Easy, Carlo, hold on!" Finley shouted.

Indian warriors moved in close to the knoll, firing several arrows at Finley's horse. The animal dropped on its haunches and labored for breath.

"Please get up, Carlo, please!" pleaded Finley. "Oh Carlo, not like this!"

A group of Indian warriors rushed first platoon. Close quarters and hand-to- hand fighting erupted on the little knoll. It was over in minutes. Sergeant Jeremiah Finley fell close to his beloved horse.

The Indians now aimed for Keogh and the other surviving C Company troopers.

There was nothing to do, but to get back to the hill with the survivors. As Keogh ordered the troopers back, Bobo appeared. The first sergeant was hatless and out of breath. He managed to pull his horse up and helped Keogh hold off the Indian warrior's advance.

"Bobo, where is Harrington?" Keogh shouted.

"I lost him, captain," said Bobo. "He was still mounted when I last saw him."

When the last of the C Company troopers made it past their position, Keogh and Bobo followed.

~

To a flat and open stretch of ground, General Custer stopped E Company. He'd gotten part of his command out of the ravine and away from the river. E Company was now below the hill, at the end of the hogback ridge. The ground gave the gray horse troop room to set up on and drive off any warriors close.

To the general's dismay, he looked behind him to see F Company running out the ravine and up the hills on foot, chased by warriors. Tom and Cooke, with some members of the headquarters unit, tried to cover the troopers.

"E Company, dismount," ordered the general. "Hohmeyer, first platoon, skirmish line, on the double! Drive those warriors back. Second platoon, cover the ridge. Horses to the middle."

Sergeant Hohmeyer took E Company's first platoon back down the hills to cover F Company and to drive the warriors approaching from the west back to the river. The second platoon with Sergeant Ogden covered the ridge to the north and east. As the E Company skirmish lines formed, warriors on the hill at the end of the hogback ridge began to fire on the troopers.

General Custer dismounted and handed his reins to Sergeant Hughes. The general, Boyer, Sharrow and Sergeant Vickory moved on foot to the edge of the flat area between the two platoons and looked to the south and east. The fate of Keogh's command was uncertain, the area completely engulfed in smoke. All they could make out were warriors everywhere.

Onto the flat area galloped Tom and Cooke, with Yates following. F Company had made it out of the ravine.

General Custer eyed the three. "We're going to take the hill at the end of the ridge and reunite with Keogh," he said. "E Company's second platoon holds here. Have Hohmeyer advance through the basin and drive out those warriors streaming into Keogh."

"My company needs ammunition," said Yates.

"Sharrow, have E Company give up some of theirs," the general ordered.

Thirty
The Stand

Indian gunfire from the south had intensified atop the hill where L Company was stationed. When Keogh and Bobo arrived, they could see that Calhoun and Crittenden had repositioned to cover the C Company retreat.

Now, the L Company skirmish line faced more to the southwest. With it doing so, the Sioux and Cheyenne approached in alarming numbers from the south and east. From the west, warriors charged the L Company line, but a succession of volleys from the company drove them back.

Keogh dismounted Comanche and scanned the terrain to the northwest for any sign of the general. He hoped for a messenger to tell him to move out what was left of his command. Nothing could be seen through the smoke. Along the hogback ridge, he could see his I Company taking a tremendous amount of gunfire, and L Company troopers to the south were being hit all around the hill.

The few C Company troopers who had made the hill gave little support. Some were without horses, many were in shock and exhausted from the run up the hill. Others were trying to fire their rifles and hold their horses at the same time. It was only a matter of time before the hill was overrun.

Think, Keogh! Think!

In his mind, he had but one choice. "Bobo, get down there to where both company's horses are being held. Get them ready to move out the second I arrive!"

"Yes, captain." The first sergeant galloped to the right, going north and east to the position where the horses were held.

Keogh moved for L Company's skirmish line. He dismounted and pulled Comanche behind Calhoun. "Gradually fall back toward us. Once we get to our horses, I'll send yours to you. We'll cover you. We've got to get out of here--- it's our only option!'"

Calhoun fired his revolver. He never took his eyes off the skirmish line. "Will do, Keogh."

Another charge by the warriors, this time by those mounted, neared the L Company line before it was repulsed. The skirmish line bunched together.

Keogh pulled himself back onto Comanche and followed by Patton, took off to the north. They followed the slope of the hill as it veered to the east. There, in the ravine, stood the horses of I and L Companies. It was time to move.

"Bobo, take L Company their horses and help Calhoun get his company mounted. Get them ready to move out on the double! Patton, keep an eye on me for the signal to horses."

"Yes, captain," said the trumpeter.

~

First Sergeant Bobo led the L Company horse holders to a position behind the L Company skirmish line. The scene was chaotic. Horses plunged and pulled against the holders. The situation worsened as several troopers broke off the line and ran for their horses.

"Stay on the line!" ordered L Company First Sergeant Butler.

"Wait, men, wait!" Lieutenant Crittenden shouted. "Stay on the line!"

"L Company, stand fast!" commanded Calhoun. "Stand fast! Stand fast, goddammit!"

"Graham!" hollered L Company Corporal William Gilbert. "Oh, Christ!"

It was too late. Private Charles Graham of L Company had taken an arrow in his back as he had thrown down his rifle and attempted to pull his revolver on several approaching warriors. The warriors moved without opposition for the left side of the L Company skirmish line.

"Shit! Sergeant Butler!" shouted Gilbert. "Pull your revolvers!"

A bullet slammed into Gilbert's thigh. As he reached for the wound, the blood running down his leg, he tried to run, but all he could manage was a hobble. An arrow then slammed into his chest and caused him to drop his revolver. He collapsed to his knees in shock, looking at the arrow resting in his chest. Two Indian warriors, one a Cheyenne and the other a Sioux, raced to count coup on the wounded trooper. After taking his scalp, the warriors took turns driving their war clubs into his head and body.

~

"Let's go, get those horses out of there!" hollered Keogh to the I Company horse holders. "Bring them on." They began pulling away from the ravine, but it was too late! To his right, warriors moved on the ridge above the I Company horses.

No! No! It can't be!

More warriors appeared from the east and began firing into the horses. The horse holders tried to pull their horses towards I Company's position, on the hogback ridge. The troopers had a choice. Either continue on amid the firing, or let the horses go and protect themselves.

Keogh stopped Comanche and looked back in the direction of L Company. Part of the company's skirmish line retreated, but was cut off by a group of mounted warriors. They were led by the warrior with the white dots over his body, riding the paint horse.

Calhoun fired his revolver and walked backwards just as his troopers on the skirmish line were smashed into by a horde of mounted warriors. Some of the troopers tried to fire while holding their horses. Others on horseback broke out and galloped north, some went south.

First Sergeant Butler tried to mount his horse amid the firing and noise. "Goddammit, Maxwell! Steady! Ho Max, ho!"

Bullets kicked up the ground all around the sergeant. When Butler's foot hit the stirrup, a bullet found the horse above his left hind leg. The horse bucked, then swung hard in a circle. The first sergeant pulled himself onto the horse as it bolted toward the river.

~

A sudden burst of gunfire tore through the air. Keogh turned to the hogback ridge to see the troopers of his I Company in trouble. Warriors had gotten too close to the I Company skirmish line.

The troopers tried to hold their ground, but there were just too many warriors. The line retreated down the slope of the hill.

Along the hogback ridge Keogh saw Bobo and his horse make an attempt at escape. The sergeant's horse took several shots and collapsed, sliding, then tumbling down the slope of the hill. From the southwest, more warriors appeared above I Company's position.

Jesus Christ! Get out of here!

Several volleys hit I Company as they retreated for their horses. Some troopers fell. Troopers Lloyd and Bailey heard the warriors as they fled. Blood and pieces of Lloyd's head splattered across Bailey's face when the bullet smashed into Lloyd's head. Lloyd's body tumbled to the ground. Bailey didn't stop.

~

In the direction of where L Company's skirmish line had once been, Keogh looked for Calhoun. The lieutenant knelt and held Crittenden as both fired their revolvers. Keogh spurred Comanche in their direction.

Keogh had to choose a target quickly as the horse carried him into the warriors. Arrows flew at Comanche, bullets whizzed by. His shots did nothing to stop the warriors closing in on Calhoun

240

and Crittenden as Comanche continued charging ahead.

"Ho boy! Ho!" shouted Keogh. He pulled the horse up as he watched Calhoun and Crittenden being overrun. Up the ridge, he witnessed Butler's horse running a gauntlet of warriors as they tried to divert the animal. The first sergeant fired his revolver but control was impossible as the horse swerved to the left and ran down the coulee.

Butler's horse ran over a rise and toward another coulee. For the moment, the shots and arrows ceased. Then the sergeant heard them---mounted warriors in pursuit!

A bullet caught Butler's horse on the back leg and the animal slowed. Butler spurred him on, yet an arrow landed in the horse's back side.

The first sergeant looked behind him. A pack of warriors split up and moved to encircle him. Butler tried to reload his revolver as he spurred the horse into the coulee. The horse staggered, then fell over hard to the right. Butler leapt as the horse went down, landing on his feet before tumbling hard to the jagged ground.

First Sergeant James Butler managed to get to his feet with his rifle close. He calmly picked up the weapon. *Bang. Bang. Bang. Bang.* The shots stopped the advancing warriors for the moment. The first sergeant was in the fight of his life and he knew it.

Sweat poured off Butler's hatless head, down across his face. With his horse gone, so was his extra ammunition. Reaching for a bullet from the belt wrapped around his waist, he realized he had but one left. His eyes darted to the left, at the warriors rushing clos-er. He aimed carefully. *Bang.* He dropped the rifle and drew his re-volver.

Heading for a rise, he ran right into a group of warriors looting his dead horse. The warriors scattered as he let loose a volley of shots. Butler turned and ran to the north, reloading the revolver without looking at it.

"Jesus Christ!" He crawled now, shot in the leg, using his elbows to pull himself into a clump of sage brush. His eyes burned with sweat and his face itched from the dirt. Pain pulsed in his leg.

Two warriors ran toward him, soon to fall after two carefully aimed shots.

The sergeant swung his body around and crouched low to face the river, scanning the area for the next safe place. He wouldn't last long on his wounded leg.

An Indian yelled, then touched Butler with a coup stick! The sergeant sprang up, exposing himself, his heart near bursting out of his chest as he fired. The third shot landed squarely in the warrior's back.

Through more sage brush, he crawled, when a bullet ripped into his right shoulder. He dropped the revolver and rolled to the left, staring at the sky. With his wounded shoulder, he struggled to push himself up. Pain from his leg and shoulder shot through his entire body. Then he heard them!

A group of warriors closed in on Butler fast. An arrow hit the sergeant in his chest. Just when he fell backward, eyes wide, the warrior smashed the rifle's butt into Butler's head. When the second arrow hit, the sergeant died.

L Company First Sergeant James Butler had sold his life dearly.

~

Keogh pulled Comanche hard to the right, he knew there was precious little time. The horse whinnied in distress, slowed and tossed his head. Keogh knew the horse had been hit. He leaned forward in the saddle to see blood running from a wound just above the front right hoof.

Comanche didn't need urged on. He raced ahead. To their front, Keogh looked up the hill at the hogback ridge where warriors poured over on horseback. "Trumpeter, to horses!" he ordered. "Blow that bugle, boy, now!"

Trumpeter Patton let go several short blasts from his bugle.

Chaos reigned all around I Company. Horses without riders ran without direction. It was hard to see through all the smoke. Keogh watched as a wave of mounted Indian warriors cut Porter's platoon off as they retreated for their horses.

"First platoon!" ordered Varden. "Get to the horses! Get the horses!"

More Indians appeared from behind I Company, to the east and the south. The warrior on the paint horse charged ahead of this group, right into the troopers. He swung his war club at any trooper he rode near. Several troopers fired on the warrior, but all missed.

Varden tried to stop the onslaught of warriors coming down on the command. He shouted, "Skirmish line! Hurry, now! First platoon, skirmish line!"

Time had run out. I Company's horses had stampeded and were gone. Keogh pulled Comanche up. Everywhere he looked, he saw nothing but Indians. I Company was completely surrounded. He turned to face his troopers, now in a semi-circle, fighting for their lives. "Come on, boy."

The only hope was to break through the ring of warriors and create a path for retreat up the hill and over the ridge.

Comanche galloped by the men of I Company. Survivors from C and L Companies had joined them now. Several were wounded, others lay dead. Varden and Bobo watched Comanche barrel ahead. The two sergeants hollered at Keogh to stop. One trooper sat in the middle of the group, crying, rocking back and forth.

When his first revolver emptied, Keogh shoved it back into the holster and grabbed a second.

Comanche took another bullet, this one in the loin. But the horse didn't stop. He struggled up the hill. Keogh could feel the horse laboring.

How much more can he give?

An Indian warrior raced to intercept him, and Keogh raised the revolver. He couldn't get his sight set.

Now!

But he never had to fire. Comanche charged ahead and ran into the Indian, sending the warrior spinning to the ground.

More warriors blocked their route. The horse kept charging ahead. Keogh fired into the group, hitting several and scattering the rest.

They found what was left of Porter's second platoon, all bunched together, many wounded. Trooper Symms and trumpeter McGucker both lay motionless in the tall grass.

It was now or never. He had to get the company reunited and over the ridge. Porter and six troopers had formed a circle, their backs to one another.

"Porter, get your wounded together. Put some fire into those warriors now, goddammit! Wait for me," Keogh ordered. He could see the lieutenant was bleeding from a gunshot wound above the shoulder.

~

F Company and the headquarters unit had driven off the warriors firing on General Custer's command. The cavalrymen took the hill at the end of the hogback ridge and planted the command's flags. Trumpeters blew the disperse signal and the troopers fanned out to take positions around the hill. They were now just over the ridge from Keogh's command.

A platoon from E Company held the right flank, down the ridge and on the flat, open area the two companies had occupied earlier. The other E Company platoon took positions below the hill to protect the company's horses.

General Custer prepared to recall Keogh's command when several small groups of troopers on horseback and some on foot, came racing out of the smoke, running to the hill. The troopers were from Keogh's command and had managed to escape the carnage. Right behind them were hundreds of warriors. Several volleys from the troopers on the hill drove the warriors back.

The hill and the entire surrounding area were now under attack. Arrows rained down on the cavalrymen. Those still in possession of their horse were ordered to shoot the animals for breastworks. The trooper's ammunition had run dangerously low.

On the right flank of the hill, a group of young Cheyenne warriors charged into the gray horse troop. Below the hill, Sioux warriors attacked E Company's other platoon. The gray horses of E Company were scattered, with some of the platoon fighting their way up to the hill where F Company and headquarters had set up. Others, made an attempt at escape by running toward the river.

~

Captain Weir and his D Company had reached the humpbacked hills. Weir took a few troopers and scrambled up to look downriver for the general's command. To their front, gunfire crackled and horsemen lined the distant ridges.

"Reno's got them coming on!" shouted Hare. The lieutenant dismounted at the base of the hill and ran up it. "He wants you to continue ahead and keep a way open."

Weir looked behind the hill he and his men occupied. He could see two, maybe three of the companies from Reno and Benteen, mounted and coming his way. Behind these, the others still organized to move out.

"Edgerly, take the troop on down and toward Custer. Keep flankers out and keep an eye on us back here," ordered Weir.

"D Troop, mount up!" shouted Edgerly.

The troopers scrambled down the hills and back to their horses. In a matter of minutes, they were on the move.

Sergeant Flanagan handed Weir his field glasses. "Here, captain, take a look. Tell me what you make of it."

~

Back down the hill, Keogh urged Comanche toward the survivors from the three companies. A warrior caught sight of him from the ridge to the west, but never fired his weapon. Instead, he raised his gunstock war club and hollered as his pony charged.

Comanche didn't wait for Keogh to lead him, the horse turned to face the assault. The two horses rushed each other. Keogh's heart raced as he raised his revolver, the distance closing. His shot missed.

Hurry!

The warrior and his pony stormed ahead. Comanche sprinted forward, not an ounce of fear in his muscles---he wasn't going to stop!

Now!

Keogh squeezed the trigger. The bullet smashed into the warrior.

He never looked back as the warrior hit the ground. He swung Comanche back down the hill, shoved the emptied revolver back into the holster and pulled another one.

When they reached what was left of the survivors, he saw Indians everywhere. Keogh emptied his revolver at those closing in. "Come on!" he shouted.

Varden rallied the men to move out. "Let's go, follow the captain. Get moving!"

Thirty troopers began to move. Some still in possession of their horses panicked and fled with no regard for their fellow troopers.

As Keogh led his men up the hill, he pulled Comanche to a stop. To the east, as if they had sprung from earth itself, more warriors poured over the ridge. A group of mounted warriors raced ahead of those on foot, straight for the cavalrymen.

"Varden!" Keogh shouted. "Behind you! Get them moving!"

He emptied another revolver at the advancing warriors and pulled Comanche hard to the left. He grabbed his last loaded revolver from his side and urged the horse to follow the troopers.

From the east and south, warriors pursued the troopers. A Sioux warrior charged on his pony, ahead of the others, straight at Keogh. There was no time for him to think. He raised his revolver.

Now.

The shot hit the warrior in the head.

A Cheyenne warrior came at Keogh now. The fury and intensity of combat surged from within Keogh. The Cheyenne hollered, trying to intimidate him. Calmly, Keogh lowered the revolver as the warrior closed in on him. The warrior intended to coup him. Keogh held the revolver at his side. "Come on! Come on!" he shouted, consumed with rage.

Bang.

The shot hit the Cheyenne in the center of his chest.

The ground kicked up all around Comanche with bullets. Arrows flew close to his side. But the horse surged ahead. Keogh tried to cover the movement of his troops, but there were too many Indians to fire on. As his revolver emptied, a group of warriors concealed by a large clump of bushes and sagebrush popped up to the right of the advancing troopers and unleashed a round of shots.

Oh my God! No!

A stinging sensation hit Keogh. A crashing pain erupted in his left leg. Comanche went down, falling over hard to the left. Keogh screamed in agony, then blacked out the moment his head hit the ground. The horse whinnied in distress and tried to regain his feet.

~

Everything went silent for Keogh as he lay where he fell. He opened his eyes and looked up at the blue sky. With the wind knocked out of him, he desperately tried to breathe.

He heard nothing.

Only the terrible pain in his left leg told him he was alive.

Varden and Bobo, with a handful of troopers fought their way to where he lay. The two sergeants formed the remaining troopers into a square around their commander. Trumpeter Patton blew the command for recall.

Varden leaned over him. "Captain!"

Keogh could not hear, but he knew what the first sergeant had said.

Bobo tied a tourniquet to Keogh's leg. He then helped him sit up. In desperation he said, "Hang on captain! Easy does it! Please hang on captain, please!"

Varden reloaded Keogh's revolvers and placed them in his hands. "They're loaded, captain."

Troopers began to fall all around those in the square now. They were being picked off with ease. Some lay dead, others dying. Those troopers not in the ring around Keogh were the first to go. Once they were wounded, the warriors rushed them and hacked the troopers to pieces.

Keogh watched helplessly as one trooper put his revolver to his own head and pulled the trigger. Keogh fired his revolvers, emptying them quickly. He closed his eyes.

You're going to die here.

As he started to lose consciousness once more, something made him raise his head. A familiar sight caught his eye amid the smoke and dust.

It was Comanche, running to escape. As the horse headed over the hogback ridge, two warriors gave chase. Keogh's heart sank as one fired his gun. The shot landed. Comanche whinnied in distress.

I'm not going to make it off this hillside alive. All of my men. Comanche. Oh, Nelly!

248

Comanche stopped running and circled on the warriors. Now, he was the hunter. He charged, reared up and kicked one warrior in the head. The blow dropped the Indian instantly. The other warrior lunged to grab Comanche's reins, the horse turned and ran him down. Comanche raised himself on his hind legs and looked in Keogh's direction.

He let out a snort and whinnied as he landed on all four feet. The horse reared again, raised himself up, and whinnied. He was telling all something. Keogh closed his eyes as he tried to hear what his horse was saying. A calm, peaceful feeling ran through him. His friend, his great horse, was saluting him, saying goodbye. Keogh opened his eyes to see the magnificent animal once more. In a flash, Comanche bolted down the other side of the hill. He was gone.

Keogh laid back and stared at the sky, his jaw clinched in pain. "Nelly, Nelly," he whispered.

Moore troopers had gone down. Indians were everywhere. An enormous roar of gunfire erupted. It found the mark squarely on the troopers surrounding Keogh.

It was all over.

Myles Keogh lay dead, his restless soul finally at peace.

Myles Keogh had just done his last dance with death.

~

Four miles away, on the humpbacked hills, Major Reno and Captain Benteen's commands joined Captain Weir's company. The officers and troopers stood and watched the black mass engulf the area where Keogh's men fought for their lives. The mass moved over the ridge, in the direction of General Custer's command.

No order was given to go to their aid.

The End

Historical Note

Readers may wonder about the historical accuracy of the events in this novel. The Battle of The Little Bighorn is the most written about battle in American history. Much that has been detailed is legend with a sprinkling of accuracy, and the same can be said for Myles Keogh's life. *A Dance With Death: An Irish Soldier of Fortune at the Little Bighorn* is a work of fiction. That said, I endeavored to stay true to history in the main events of the story.

What is for certain is that Myles Keogh did leave his home in Ireland to fight for the Pope. After the Papal war, he and his two comrades did come to America to fight in the Civil War. Then, Keogh received a commission as Captain of Company I, United States Seventh Cavalry. He remained as such until his death at the Battle of The Little Bighorn on June 25, 1876.

Along his life's incredible journey, Myles Keogh did meet Nelly Martin and Comanche. It is up to the reader to decide what is fact or fiction.

Acknowledgments

Many friends who have studied the Battle of the Little Bighorn gave freely of their time to help with this novel. Some live near the battlefield still today; others come and we converge there every week on the battle's anniversary to study, talk and wonder how this tragic event played out. To these great people, I owe so much. Thank you, Thank you!

Thanks to these wonderful historians and researchers on the Battle of the Little Bighorn: Bob Snelson, Chris Dixon, Tim Baum, Will Hutchison, Richard Upton, Mike O'Keefe, Mike Koury, Vince Heier, Don Fisk, Tom Heski, John Doerner, Ron Nichols, Sandy Bernard, Jim Donovan, Mark Gardner, Danny Martinez, Steve Andrews, Gordon Richard, Albert Winkler, Randy Tucker and John Koster.

A sincere thanks to National Park Service, Little Bighorn National Monument Park Ranger Michael Donahue. Without Mike's incredible knowledge of this battle and his time answering all my questions, this author would have never have stood a chance at getting part of it right.

Thanks to these incredible folks who live near the battlefield. They have given so freely of their time, stories and friendship: Faron Iron, Linwood Tallbull, Dennis Limberhand, Clara Caufield, Donovan Taylor, Wallace Bearchum, Alden Bigman Jr., Putt Thompson, Judd Thompson, Patrick Hill and Carla Colstad.

Most importantly, a special thanks to my family. Thank you, Melinda, for putting up with me as I chased this story all these years. I love you. Thanks to my aunt, Jeanie Pillen, my uncle, Bill Scott and my brother, Bryan, who all listened and read my work. Thank you to Jim Page and Dr. Brad Lookingbill for their encouragement. A sincere thanks to Kaitlyn Johnson, my editor, and to Neal Von Flue for the cover design of the book. Lastly, thanks to Matthew Wayne Selznick for getting this book published and out to the world.

Printed in Great Britain
by Amazon